ALOHA REUNION
Debby Mayne

College senior Leilani is blind-sided by the emotional impact of Jeff Sorenson's arrival in Hawaii. Her physical attraction to him is evident from the moment he steps off the plane with his sister Betty, who has returned for a reunion of old school roommates.

Jeff has a history of being a ladies' man, so Leilani tries to guard her heart. But Jeff joins the group in a mudsliding adventure, and then he manages to get Leilani alone in the waves at Waikiki, where they're nearly an even match at bodysurfing. No matter how much she fights her feelings, she's unable to resist his charms, and when he sweeps her off her feet, she knows she can't stop herself from falling completely and totally in love with Jeff.

There's only one problem: Jeff lives in Arizona and Leilani's future is in Hawaii.

ALOHA REUNION

•

Debby Mayne

AVALON BOOKS
NEW YORK

PRINTED IN THE UNITED STATES OF AMERICA
ON ACID-FREE PAPER
BY HADDON CRAFTSMEN, BLOOMSBURG, PENNSYLVANIA

This book is dedicated to my daughters,
Alison and Lauren, and my husband, Wally.

Acknowledgments

Thanks to editors Erin Cartwright, Mira Son, and Susan McCarty for all your hard work on this book. Also, thanks to Kathy Carmichael, Kim Llewellyn, and Tara Spicer for providing support and being such great friends.

Chapter One

"Leilani, my brother Jeff is flying with me to Hawaii," Betty said in her e-mail. "He's staying with friends, so you probably won't see much of him. Tell Deanne that I have the pictures already packed, so she doesn't have to worry. And no matter how tempting it is to tell the rest of them, let Jeff's visit be a surprise to everyone." She went on and on about her flight plans and mentioned some of the things she wanted to do while back in Hawaii. She closed with a simple, "Aloha, Betty."

As Leilani signed off, she let out a deep sigh. She had found out about this house from Betty during one of their classes together at the University of Hawaii. The house was fine, although quite small, and it had barely enough room for four women.

1

Debby Mayne

There were two bedrooms, each with two twin beds and very little in the way of decoration. There simply wasn't enough room. The living room had a couch, two chairs, and a rabbit-eared thirteen-inch television that came with the place. In the kitchen, there was a table with six chairs, which meant that two of them could have guests for dinner, if they were all there. There was no dining room, but that didn't matter. This wasn't a formal arrangement for anyone. It was just a convenient place to live with a bunch of really nice people.

Leilani knew Betty's brother Jeff from the many times he'd come around. In fact, after she got over gawking at how wonderful he was to look at, she began to see him as a slightly older, really hunky guy she could only dream about because when they'd gone out, he'd kept her at arm's length. At times, though, she caught him staring at her when they were in a group, and she just smiled, trying to ignore her pulse that quickened at his gaze. She knew she was attracted to him, but she didn't see that she had a chance.

They had gone out a few times, but Leilani didn't think Jeff took their dating seriously. Right after their third date, he'd shown up at a party with a pretty coed on his arm. That hadn't lasted long, and before she knew it, there was someone else. It was painfully obvious that she wasn't special to Jeff and that he just wanted to have fun, so she'd taken a step back whenever he was around.

Leilani's main attraction to Jeff, besides his looks of course, had been the way he made everyone feel comfortable. He had an amazing ability to be everyone's friend. She'd never seen him in a situation he couldn't handle. She'd always been a quiet person in the group, so she admired his outgoing nature and ability to hold a crowd in the palm of his hand.

Since she was an only child, Leilani was the center of her family's attention. Sure, she was considered spoiled by her cousins who came from homes with as many as a half dozen siblings, but she had a very strong sense of doing the right thing. Just because she didn't have to share her toys with sisters and brothers, they teased her about being an only child. And she found herself trying to prove them wrong.

Leilani was half *haole* and half Hawaiian. She was considered a local, which for most people meant living at home while going to college to save expenses; but her parents encouraged her to get out on her own for her last two years of college.

Deanne came into the kitchen where Leilani had already flipped the switch on the coffeemaker. "Heard from Betty yet?"

Leilani knew Betty wanted to keep Jeff's visit a secret, but she could say anything else she wanted to without blowing the surprise. "Yes," she said.

"Everything is still on. Her flight has been confirmed, and she wants to make sure we have plenty of *saimin* and crack seed."

"I sent her some for Christmas," Deanne said. "But she said it doesn't taste the same on mainland soil."

Leilani laughed. "I'm sure that's right. A lot of things are different when you're here."

"I bet she forgets the pictures."

"No," Leilani said. "She told me she already has them packed, so don't worry."

"That's good," Deanne said as she jumped up and headed for the door. "Gotta run. Can't keep the customers waiting." She rented surfboards to tourists part-time while she was working on her graduate degree in computer science. Everyone teased her about that, calling her a surfer geek. "How's Betty getting here?"

"I'll pick them up at the airport," Leilani said.

"Them?" Deanne said, pausing with her hand on the knob, looking perplexed.

"Uh, her, I mean." Leilani didn't see why it was a big deal to keep it a secret, but she didn't want to be the one to let the cat out of the bag about Jeff coming.

"I figured you were talking about Sally."

"Sally?" Leilani knew that Sally wasn't due to arrive for a few days.

"I thought maybe Sally was able to get her flight switched."

"No, she tried, but everything's booked solid." Whew! Looked like she almost blew it, but now she was off the hook.

After Deanne left, Leilani sat at the table and sipped her coffee while she thought about their plans to go to a concert at Kapiolani Park and maybe even take a hike near Diamond Head. Because Leilani and her roommates were students, funds were limited, and they had to find cheap, creative ways to have fun. It wasn't hard, though, because the ocean and sand were free, and they managed to make at least one meal a day from a bowl of *saimin*, an oriental noodle in a broth base.

The next few days dragged by, but the arrival date for Betty and her brother was finally here. Leilani pulled on one of her basic muumuus and slid into her everyday slippers, thong sandals she wore everywhere.

Her tiny compact car managed to run on fumes most of the time, but since she didn't know where Jeff was staying, she put a little more gas in the tank. It wouldn't be cool to run out of gas and strand their guests out on the highway, pushing her car to the nearest gas station.

Traffic on the airport road was running smoothly, so she had time to stop at the lei stands and pick up a couple of plumeria leis. Since flowers were in abundance, they were the cheapest offering available, yet they were just as pretty as anything else.

Leilani stood at the terminal gate and waited, looking forward to seeing Betty again. It had been almost a year since Betty had graduated, so she knew they'd have quite a bit to talk about. She hoped she didn't get tongue-tied around Jeff. Fortunately, she wasn't known for being a big talker, so no one would notice if she didn't say much.

The plane arrived on time. Leilani had the perfect spot to watch the passengers disembark. She spotted Betty before Betty saw her. The mainland had really changed her friend.

Before, when living in Hawaii, Betty's favorite outfit was a pair of denim cutoffs, a tank top, and slippers. She wore her shoulder-length hair clipped in a barrette, no makeup on her face. Now, though, she had on a white linen suit, a face that was made up to perfection, and styled hairdo. Leilani shrank back as she thought about what she was wearing. The only makeup she'd bothered with was a light touch of coral-colored lipstick. Her hair was long, and it hung to her waist, showing that she hadn't been to a hairdresser in years. In Hawaii, a beauty shop could go out of business if they depended on college students to make a living.

"Lani!" Betty called the second she spotted Leilani. She was into nicknames, shortening anyone's name if she spotted an opportunity.

"Aloha, Betty," Leilani said as she draped the flower lei around her friend's neck. Betty gave her a hug, which she returned. It felt mighty good to see her old friend again.

Jeff was right behind his sister, grinning from ear to ear. His blond hair, blue eyes, and brightly colored shirt made him seem more at home in this place than Betty.

He reached for Leilani before she had a chance to greet him. "How's the cutest little Hawaiian girl I know?" he asked as he gave her a warm hug. His crooked smile and easy manner put her nerve endings in high gear.

Leilani had almost forgotten about the lei she'd brought for Jeff. Obviously, he'd seen it dangling from her wrist because he tilted his head toward her.

She dropped it around his neck and turned to give him a quick peck on the cheek as was customary. What she didn't expect was the way he kissed her back. The quick surge of attraction rendered her knees weak, as if the bone had been replaced by jelly. Suddenly, she felt the impact of the schoolgirl crush she'd once had on him.

Jeff's mouth went dry the instant he spotted Leilani waiting for him and his sister, the flower leis draped from her arm. She was as beautiful as ever.

Her touch was soft and tender, just as he'd remembered it, and it had taken every ounce of self-restraint to not pull her into his embrace for a longer, deeper kiss. But Betty would have killed him.

One thing he remembered loving about Leilani was how she would quietly sit in a group of people as they chattered on and on. She paid rapt attention to everything, which was why she was the most intelligent woman there. Intelligent women were his big weakness, and from what he could tell, Leilani was hands down the most brilliant of any woman he'd known.

Leilani looked at Jeff and wondered what was on his mind. He'd been staring at her for several seconds, sending tingles up her arms and down her spine.

Betty's chortle brought Leilani back to the moment. "So, how's everything going, Lani?"

"It's going. How about with you?"

With a shrug, Betty replied, "Same here. I sure do wish I was living back here. Banking is such a stuffy business, I find myself wanting to return to the casual lifestyle of Hawaii so I can feel good again."

"You don't feel good?" Leilani asked with concern.

"I feel okay, I guess. But I miss the warm sunshine, the walks on the beach at sunset, and the smells. Did you know that Hawaii has its own distinct smell?"

Leilani laughed. "I'm sure it does with all these people around."

Jeff managed to work his way in between his sister and Leilani. He guided them over to the baggage claim area. "Betty packed everything but her ironing board. I'm sure she would have brought that, too, but it wouldn't have fit in my car."

"I wanted to make sure I had what I needed," Betty said, nudging her brother in the side.

"All you need here is a swimsuit, a muumuu, and some slippers," Leilani said.

Jeff nodded. "That's what I told her. I have shorts and comfortable shirts mostly. I did bring a couple pairs of long pants, just in case we go somewhere nice."

Leilani cast a quick glance over at Jeff. "Where are you staying while you're here?" Man, was he good looking! And as if that weren't enough, his smile undid her from the inside out.

"Some of the guys I used to hang with have settled down and bought houses. I'm staying with a married buddy who has a place near Diamond Head. It looks pretty cool in the pictures." She felt Jeff's gaze on her as he spoke, and her heart did that double turn again. *Time to get a grip,* she told herself.

"Sounds nice." Jeff's nearness had rendered her nearly speechless, so she had to force herself to hold up her end of the conversation. "So what's the plan?" she asked, hoping she wouldn't have to say much more. She'd make a total fool of herself.

"I thought I'd check out my buddy's place for a while, until he and his wife get tired of me. Then I'll head over to Aiea and stay with another friend." Jeff was friendly, so it was no surprise that he had more friends than Leilani could count.

He went on about his friend who'd gotten a job teaching high school English and the fact that he'd only heard his friend speak pidgin, a simple combination of English and Hawaiian. "I didn't even know he could speak proper English, let alone teach it. I guess it just goes to prove a guy can change."

That's for sure, Leilani thought. One look at Jeff told her that. And his changes were all for the better.

Jeff Sorenson had always been really good looking. He had the confidence of someone much older, too, which she found alluring. She'd often watched him as he teased the other roommates and wondered why he didn't talk to her like he did them. She was the youngest one in the group, so maybe that was it. He didn't know her as well.

What seemed the most different, though, was the maturity she now saw in his eyes, which only enhanced his looks. He seemed to know exactly what he wanted and where he was going. She knew he was intelligent and had heard that he was sought after by every corporation in the country because of his computer savvy. He was able to analyze information faster than anyone else, making him a valuable asset to any company.

Jeff Sorenson seemed bigger than life when she heard updates about him, yet he was so down-to-earth in person. His eyes looked directly into hers when he spoke to her, making her feel like she was the most important person on earth.

Betty touched Leilani's arm. "I can't believe how I already feel, Lani. This place is so incredible. I want to live here again."

"Why don't you?" Leilani asked. "You can get a transfer or something." She would have loved nothing more than for Betty to return. She missed all those late-night gab sessions and words of wisdom that only Betty could impart.

Nodding, Betty replied, "I just might do that. But I'm sure it'll be close to impossible with everyone wanting to be here."

"Maybe not," Jeff said. "This place is so expensive, many people are trying to get back to the mainland so they have money left over after paying their bills."

"True," Betty agreed. "But the lifestyle here is so wonderful. Who needs money?"

Jeff chuckled. "Only those who need a lot of toys to keep them happy."

Leilani noticed how they were talking as if she weren't there. They must have had a discussion about this on the plane, making her think that possibly one or both of them had been thinking seriously about coming back to Hawaii. This brought a smile to her lips.

"Got plans for tonight?" Jeff asked as they got into her tiny car. He'd effortlessly hoisted the luggage into the trunk and made it fit, although Leilani was concerned when she first saw the number of suitcases Betty had brought.

She started to shake her head. What was he asking? Did he mean her or the whole group?

Betty saved the moment. "Jeff wants to treat everyone to dinner at the Outrigger."

Leilani didn't eat out at nice restaurants very often, so she quickly nodded. "I'm sure everyone will be delighted."

"I'm sure," Betty said with a flash of amusement. "College students never turn down a free meal. I know I never did."

This was true. Ever since Leilani had moved out of her parents' modest but comfortable home, she found that she appreciated some of the things she'd come to take for granted. That was probably why her folks had encouraged her to get out on her own for a couple of years. They were nearby, so she knew she wouldn't starve. But they weren't right there, always ready to catch her if she fell. She had to be industrious and creative in order to have any fun at all. Fortunately, that wasn't hard to do in Hawaii.

"Is Deanne seeing anyone?" Jeff asked. "That woman always liked having a man on her arm. She didn't like to go anywhere alone."

Leilani's heart sank. Jeff was interested in Deanne. She should have figured that out a long time ago. They were both equally gorgeous, outgoing, and smart.

"No, I think she's between guys right now. She has a few more months of computer programming, and then she goes into her internship."

Jeff nodded. "I'm the one who talked her into majoring in computer programming. She's a natural."

Sure, she was. And she also was a natural to have a man like Jeff, Leilani thought.

"Do you know where she's planning to intern?" Jeff asked.

Leilani shrugged. "I'm not sure. Several companies have offered her an opportunity, but I think she's still deciding."

"The company I used to work for is one of them," Jeff said. "I told them about her."

Yes, she should have figured this out from the beginning. Betty had said to keep Jeff's visit a surprise, and she'd heard Deanne talk about Jeff nonstop. Deanne had said that Jeff was like a big brother to her, but Leilani was beginning to wonder if that was a cover for her true feelings.

Disappointment clouded her mind; she missed her turn off the main road. Betty reached over and touched Leilani's arm. "Weren't you supposed to turn back there? Or has something changed that I don't know about?"

"Oh, yeah," Leilani said as she did a U-turn in the middle of the road, which was easy to do in her small car. "I wasn't paying attention."

Jeff was sitting in the backseat not making a sound. Leilani then remembered that she might need to take him someplace.

"Where're you staying, Jeff? Didn't you say someplace near Diamond Head?" she asked, looking at him in her rearview mirror. "I can take you there." Good thing she got gas, or she wouldn't have been able to make that offer.

"Don't worry about it," he replied. "I can call my buddy from your place."

"You sure?"

Jeff nodded. "I want to see the ladies." She glanced in the rearview mirror and caught his teasing grin.

Betty belted out a deep laugh. "And I'm sure the ladies want to see you, too, Jeff." She turned to Leilani and added, "You never really did get to know my brother very well, did you, Lani?"

Shaking her head, Leilani replied, "No, not very

well." She was around him a lot, but only in a group after their few dates.

"That's because you wouldn't let me," he said to Betty. Jeff's voice came from the backseat, clear as a bell. "We'll have to do something to change that." Was he teasing her, or did he really mean it?

Leilani's hand slipped from the steering wheel, but she caught herself before she did something stupid or dangerous. Why was her heart beating out of control, just because Jeff made a comment about getting to know her? Was she being silly, or what?

This ridiculous schoolgirl attraction toward her friend's brother had to stop, she thought. They'd be here for two weeks, and she could really make an idiot of herself if she didn't get a grip.

Betty gasped when the house came into view. "The place hasn't changed a bit," she said as her eyes teared up. Leilani was a little surprised at Betty's reaction. Gone was the cool professional image she'd projected when she first stepped off the plane.

Jeff snickered. "What did you expect? Did you think it would grow into a mansion or something?"

"It's so . . . so . . ." Betty wasn't able to finish her sentence because she was still choked up and misty-eyed.

"So small?" Jeff offered. He grinned at Leilani.

Houses near the university campus were in high demand, regardless of their size. It was nearly impossible for new students to find a convenient place to live. That was why she had to jump on the opportunity that Betty had offered. She knew she'd never have anything like this fall in her lap again.

Jeff was the first one out of the car when she pulled into the driveway. Betty was a little slower to get out, Leilani noticed, taking the time to savor the moment.

"Where is everyone?" Jeff asked once they were inside. "I was expecting a greeting committee."

"You would," Betty replied. She glanced sideways at Leilani, shook her head, then turned back to Jeff. "The whole island doesn't stop just because you decided to grace the place with your presence."

"Okay, okay," Jeff said, backing away. "I'm just a little disappointed. I've waited a long time to see everyone and I thought they might be here."

"I thought so, too," Leilani admitted. "But you'll see 'em later."

"I have to admit, I'm a little surprised Deanne isn't here waiting," Betty said. "I figured she'd at least wanna see my brother."

Leilani smiled at her. "You told me not to mention that Jeff was coming."

"Oh yeah, that's right."

"Are they all in class?" Jeff asked as he leaned against the door frame.

"Terri and Marlene are," Leilani replied. "Deanne's at work."

"Is she still renting surfboards?" Jeff asked.

"When she's not in class, she's either at the computer lab or at the surfboard stand."

"Figures." Jeff pulled away from the door, walked around, and looked at all the new pictures on the walls. It was tradition for each new roommate to add to the picture gallery, showing all the important moments of their lives. Leilani had one of her wearing a grass skirt, snapped during her hula class back in elementary school. She saw him pause and smile at that picture. "Cute." He turned and paused before saying, "Someone needs to tell Deanne that all work and no play will make her crazy."

"Yeah," Betty quipped. "You've never had that problem, have you, Jeff?"

"Never," he said with a grin.

Just then, the front door opened, and Deanne walked in. Everyone stopped talking and stared as Jeff turned, smiled, and made his move. Within seconds, he and Deanne were hugging. Leilani's heart felt like it had just fallen out of her chest.

Chapter Two

"Hey, rug rat," Jeff said, stepping back from Deanne and taking a long look at her, with everyone else watching, smiling. "You don't know when to quit working, do you?"

Deanne's hand went to her hair, smoothing it down. Her face was flushed. "I didn't know you were coming, Jeff," she said, her voice barely audible.

Leilani studied her roommate and felt her heart sink even further. There was definitely something going on between these two.

"You didn't ask," he said, offering a dopey grin. "Besides, I wanted it to be a surprise." He turned to Leilani and winked. "Thanks for not saying anything."

18

Deanne turned to Leilani and glared at her. "You knew?"

Slowly, Leilani nodded. "Yeah, I knew." She frowned at Jeff. "And thanks a lot for telling on me."

He offered her a mock salute. "Think nothing of it." Leaning toward her, he whispered, "She'll get over it." Her skin tingled as his breath brushed over her cheek. She couldn't have talked if she'd wanted to.

As the four of them headed toward the kitchen, Leilani dropped back and watched the others chatter and laugh like the old friends they were. Deanne was obviously overjoyed at the fact that Jeff was here.

Betty turned and offered an understanding smile. Leilani forced herself to grin back, but she felt like the odd one out. Betty was always the type to smooth things over; in fact, she often acted like a mother hen, keeping her little chicks in line.

Leilani had known Betty for almost a year before Betty graduated. They'd had several classes together, and they'd eaten lunch in the snack shop on campus. Their friendship formed fast because the chemistry between them was good. Leilani loved Betty's easy way of dealing with life and being organized. She seemed so in control, contrasting how Leilani felt most of the time. At least Leilani knew she could count on Betty to understand her feelings.

"Did you ever ditch that Ryan guy?" Leilani heard Jeff ask Deanne. "He was a loser."

She gave him a playful shove. "He was not a loser."

"No," Jeff said, turning on his California accent, "I don't, like, guess he's like, a winner, either."

"He was a professional athlete," Deanne argued.

"Yeah, like I consider the first runner up in a state surfing contest a professional athlete." Jeff turned and winked again at Leilani, which had her puzzled. Why did he even look at her when he was obviously interested in Deanne? "What's he doing now?"

Deanne grinned sheepishly. "He flips burgers at Happy's."

Jeff lifted his hands, palms up. "There ya go, every professional athlete's dream."

"He's still trying to make the surfing circuit, and they give him flexibility with his schedule."

Nodding, Jeff said, "Sounds to me like you have a lot of confidence in your boyfriend."

"Oh, he's not my boyfriend," Deanne quipped. "I told him to hit the road last month."

Jeff laughed, dropping Leilani's spirits even more. "Who's the lucky guy this week?"

Deanne shrugged. "I don't have time for anyone now. I'm almost finished with my academic work, and Steve has me working a lot at the beach."

Leilani figured that was an open door that Jeff would surely enter. But he didn't. He reached out and gave Deanne a brotherly pat on the shoulder and said, "I'm sure Mr. Right is out there somewhere. You've never gone long without someone by your side, so I have a feeling that when you're ready, you'll find the perfect guy."

Letting out a long sigh, Deanne said, "That used to be a lot more important to me than it is now."

Jeff backed up to where he'd been standing beside Leilani, cupped his hand in front of his mouth like he was about to tell her a secret, and said loud enough for Deanne to hear, "That's what she says now, but we all know better."

Deanne pretended to be offended, but it was obvious that she wasn't. In fact, she started laughing with Jeff.

"Okay, let me make a few phone calls, and I'll be out of your hair for a few hours." He glanced back and forth between Deanne and Leilani. "And tonight, I'm taking you all to the Outrigger for dinner. That is, if the others want to join us."

"I'm sure they will," Deanne squealed with excitement. "It's about time we had something besides peanut butter sandwiches and *saimin*."

Leilani just stood there and smiled. Jeff was an incredible guy who had an amazing ability to capture everyone's attention yet seem to be humble at the same time. His greatest asset was also his biggest flaw because it was hard to tell what he was really thinking, since he treated everyone the same.

But when those eyes of his were focused on her, she felt like the only woman in the room. She knew she needed to get over this feeling, or it would wind up being the longest two weeks of her life. Besides, jealousy wasn't an emotion that looked good on anyone, and she was afraid that she'd show it if he decided he wanted to be with someone while he was here.

"Phone in the same place?" Jeff asked.

It took a second before Leilani realized he'd directed the question to her. She nodded.

Betty had steered Deanne and Leilani to the living room, where she was telling her old roommates about her job. "It's really a pretty good deal," she said, "if you don't mind the corporate way of life."

"I don't see how you can get away from that in banking," Deanne said. "And since you majored in finance, you're stuck."

With a chuckle, Betty went on, "I've put in for a transfer to Hawaii, but I'm not holding my breath."

"That would be so cool!" Deanne cooed. "Just the thought of having the whole gang back is cool. How about Jeff? Any chance he might do the same thing?"

Betty shrugged. "He's looking into it too. Jeff's situation is a lot more flexible than mine, though, so it shouldn't be too difficult for him. He's self-employed now, even though he spends most of his time at one company. If he can get a couple of decent accounts here and talk his big contract company into letting him work out of a remote office, there's nothing to stand in his way."

Leilani instantly glanced at Deanne to see her reaction. Deanne looked back at her and smiled. "Jeff has always done exactly what he wants to do. He just makes other people think things were their own bright ideas."

"Yeah," Betty agreed. "My brother is a champion manipulator. I like having him for a big brother, but I worry about him in the romance department."

Deanne nodded her agreement. "Yeah, falling in love with Jeff is like jumping out of a plane without a parachute."

Leilani's ears rang. Was Deanne referring to her own feelings, or was she just making a general statement? She wasn't going to take a chance either way. Staying away from Jeff would be the only way to keep her own heart intact. He was the first guy she'd met in a long time who'd managed to get her nerves in such a jumbled mess. In fact, he was the only guy who'd done that just by sitting in the backseat of her car.

It wasn't long before Jeff came out of the kitchen with a huge grin on his face. "Anthony's coming to get me. He wants to see Betty."

"I thought he got married," Betty said, flustered. It was the first time Leilani had ever seen her this way.

49106

"That doesn't mean he's dead," Jeff replied. "Besides, the two of you haven't been together in almost three years. You're just friends now, remember?"

"Oh, yeah," she said unconvincingly. "That's right."

"Let's get my stuff out of your trunk," Jeff said to Leilani.

She followed him outside with her keys. As soon as they were behind her car, he turned and faced her. "I didn't want to ask you in front of everyone, in case you wanted to say no . . ." His voice trailed off, and he studied her face for a moment.

"What did you want to ask me?" Leilani said.

"Would you like to go to the beach with me tomorrow afternoon? My sister said you like to bodysurf, and I haven't done that in a long time. Anthony's gotta work tomorrow, so I figured I'd rent a car and we could kind of hang out a little, while I'm here."

"You want to hang out with me?" Leilani asked, wondering why he'd asked her rather than Deanne.

"Well, yeah, if you don't have anything else going on for the next couple of weeks." His face looked like that of an expectant child who'd just asked for something he knew he couldn't have.

Not wanting to seem too anxious, Leilani shrugged and said, "Well, I guess that'd be okay. I don't have many plans."

Jeff gave her the warmest smile she'd ever seen, his eyes crinkling at the corners of his still-tanned face. "Good. I was hoping you'd say that."

Leilani bit her lip as she thought about what Jeff had asked her to do. She knew she needed to remind herself that he was only asking her for companionship while he was here. Nothing else.

"We were talking about going mudsliding in a few days if the conditions are right," Leilani said, sticking her neck out but not feeling like it was too big of a risk since he'd already asked her out. Well, sort of asked her out. Going bodysurfing wasn't exactly considered a date, but then neither would mudsliding, since it was with the whole group.

"Mudsliding?" Jeff said in happy surprise. "I haven't done that in a long time. Years, in fact."

"Me, neither," Leilani admitted. "But we thought it would be fun."

He leveled his gaze on her. "I can't think of anything that would be more fun than sliding in the mud with you."

Leilani had to look down quickly to keep him from seeing what she was thinking. Jeff had an amazing ability to render her both speechless and transparent. He used the combined elements of surprise and flattery to relate to her, something he did with every female. She needed to guard her heart, or she'd surely lose it to him.

"Anthony's gonna let me borrow his van tonight,

so I can pick you all up to go to the Outrigger." Jeff had pulled his things from her trunk and was now looking directly down at her.

His close proximity took her breath away. She had to turn slightly to find her voice.

Leilani nodded. "Sounds good. Sure you don't want me to drive?"

"I'm sure. You can't fit everyone in that little car of yours, and I think it would be a lot more fun if we all went together."

"Is Anthony coming to dinner with us?" Leilani had met him once, years ago, and he'd seemed like a very nice guy.

"No, I don't think so," Jeff replied, shaking his head. "His wife already made plans for tonight, and Anthony isn't about to upset her. She's pregnant with twins."

"Oh." Leilani smiled. "How far along?"

"Several months . . . I'm not sure."

"And they already know they're having twins?"

Jeff laughed. "When the doctor picked up a second heartbeat, he ordered an ultrasound. They just found out last week. I'm gonna try not to get in their way too much, since I'm sure Pua is beside herself with this pregnancy."

"I don't think I ever met Pua."

"No, you probably haven't. She and Anthony were high school sweethearts, but they split up when he went to college. They thought they wouldn't have anything in common anymore. But true love has a way of bringing people together, whether they think they have something in common or not." Jeff looked at her tenderly and smiled. Leilani grinned back, but looked away as soon as she could without making Jeff think something was going on.

All this talk of true love made Leilani uncomfortable. She'd once thought she was in love, but sometime during her first year of college, the feeling had faded, leaving her empty and thinking there had to be more to a relationship than what she had. Obviously, her boyfriend had felt it, too, because he'd been the one to do the breaking up. Leilani had been relieved.

Jeff piled his suitcases on the front porch, ready for Anthony's arrival. Leilani went inside so she wouldn't be so obvious in how she felt. Deanne rarely missed anything, and she didn't feel like answering too many questions. Not yet, anyway.

The one who seemed aware of the fact that she'd been gone for a while was Betty, who cast a quick glance when she came out and joined the group. "Anthony here yet?" Betty asked slowly, her eyes narrowing with understanding.

"Not yet," Leilani replied. "He'll be here any minute."

Betty headed toward the door. "I need to find out what time we're leaving so I can take my shower."

Deanne tilted her head. "Don't you want to see Anthony?"

"N-no," Betty stuttered, sounding out of character for the composed woman she generally was. "Better not."

Leilani knew that Betty had once had very strong feelings, probably stronger than Jeff realized, for her brother's best friend. What a tangled web this was, she thought. All sorts of relationships going every which way. This certainly would be an interesting vacation.

Since Deanne and Betty had shared a room before, Leilani offered to give up her bed for the two weeks Betty would be staying with them, thinking the old roommates would want to share again.

"No way," Betty said. "I'll take the futon. You had to sleep on it your first semester here. I wouldn't dream of taking your bed."

"I really don't mind," Leilani said.

"I said no. Besides, I want to take turns sleeping in both bedrooms. That way, I can catch up on what's going on."

Deanne giggled and nodded toward Leilani. "That won't last long after she spends one night in Marlene and Terri's room. She's obviously forgotten that they don't turn out the light until the sun starts to rise."

"I haven't forgotten," Betty said as she pulled a

sleep mask from her overnight bag. "That's why I brought this."

"If you change your mind about the bed," Leilani offered again, "just let me know. I really don't mind."

"Thanks, Lani." Betty glanced at her watch. "I hope you don't mind if I go ahead and take a shower. With one bathroom, I'm afraid we won't all have time to get ready for dinner."

"Go right ahead," Deanne said. "I'll go next. It was hot on the beach today, and not many people wanted to rent a board. I'd much rather be busy." She turned to Leilani and smiled, tilting her head. "Can I have a few minutes of your time?"

"Uh, sure," Leilani replied. "Wanna go out to the back porch?"

"Okay," Deanne said as she headed toward the front door without waiting.

"What's up?" Leilani asked once they were outside.

"You like Jeff?" Deanne looked at her plainly after the jolting question.

Leilani felt strange. What should she say? Tell the truth and admit her strong attraction? Or should she lie to save face?

She'd hesitated a moment too long. "That's what I thought," Deanne said. "I have a chance to go out with a new guy I just met after dinner tonight, but I wasn't sure if I should, since Jeff's here. Now that

I know you're interested in him, I won't feel so guilty for abandoning the group."

"I don't want to cut in on anything you already have going with Jeff," Leilani said, her voice cracking.

Deanne belted out a laugh. "Hey, don't worry. Jeff and I tried the romance thing years ago. It doesn't work between us. I'm too flighty, and he's too into being Mr. Professional."

"You sure?" Leilani asked, suddenly feeling hope and a huge sense of relief.

"Positive," Deanne reassured her. "If you weren't interested in Jeff, I figured I could take him off your hands and keep him busy after dinner tonight. I saw the way he looked at you."

"You did?" Leilani asked. "He was looking at me?"

"Looking at you isn't exactly a strong enough statement. He was ogling you."

It was Leilani's turn to laugh. *Ogling?* She hardly thought that was an accurate description of what he was doing. But still, it made her feel pretty good, or at least, less insecure.

"Jeff seems like a really good guy," Leilani finally commented, unable to come up with anything brilliant to say about him.

"Yes, he is definitely a good guy. I think the two of you should hit it off."

So now, with Deanne's blessing, Leilani could

enjoy the evening and not feel like she had to worry about competition. A heavy burden lifted from her shoulders, just knowing this.

The sound of Marlene and Terri's voices grew louder as they came up the sidewalk. Deanne leaned back and yelled, "Hey, Betty, Marlene and Terri are here."

Betty came running out to embrace her old friends. She'd showered and changed into something more casual. Deanne excitedly told the other two roommates about Jeff's invitation to dinner. They both squealed about Jeff coming with Betty and the great meal he would treat them to at the Outrigger.

"Go get ready," Betty said. "I'm starved."

There was barely enough time for all of them to shower and dress before Jeff came back to pick them up. "Nice wheels," Betty said. "Is this what married men with kids on the way drive these days?"

Jeff looked at his sister with compassion. "Apparently." Then, he turned to the rest of the women. "Someone sit up front with me. Leilani?"

"Go ahead, Lani," Betty said. "You're the only one who won't get into a battle of wills with my brother."

"That's right," Jeff mumbled. "Betty's making me behave around you."

"Really?" Leilani said, glancing over her shoulder at her old friend.

"Yeah," Betty admitted. "Remember, my brother was always the heartbreaker type. I didn't want to lose any friends."

"You never worried about me," Deanne quipped.

"That's because you and Jeff were cut from the same cloth," Betty rapidly replied. "You can take care of yourselves."

Jeff cleared his throat and corrected his sister. "I have a feeling Leilani can do a pretty good job of taking care of herself too."

Was that a compliment? Leilani wondered. She wanted it to be. She slid into the front seat of Anthony's car and fastened her seatbelt as the others got in the side door. It sure was nice of Anthony to loan Jeff his car.

"I've been craving some fresh mahi mahi," Jeff said once they were on their way.

Leilani grinned back at him. "Sounds good to me too."

"You can have anything you want," he said softly so only she could hear him.

Those simple words gave Leilani a thrill like none she'd ever experienced before. If he only knew how many ways she could take them. She was sure he only meant from the restaurant menu, although she wanted to believe otherwise—that he was available for her if she wanted to be with him.

Chapter Three

Jeff held the chairs for each woman who sat on either side of him. "I'm so honored to be able to share this experience with you ladies."

"Cut the lines, big brother," Betty warned. "We know you too well."

"Maybe Leilani doesn't." He looked hurt, but it was obvious he was acting silly for her benefit.

"Then it's high time we warned her." Betty turned to Leilani and grinned as she leaned toward her. "My big brother is full of himself. Don't listen to a thing he says. As long as you keep this in mind, he can be a lot of fun. Just don't take him seriously."

Leilani forced a laugh. "I'll try to remember that."

Jeff groaned. "I can't believe my own sister would do something this cruel."

"It's for your own good, Jeff." Betty picked up her water glass and took a few sips before turning to the others. "Okay, so tell me who you're all dating now."

Deanne rolled her eyes and grinned when all eyes turned to her. "Why is everyone looking at me? Do you think I'm some sort of weirdo, or something?"

"That's beside the point," Betty said with a laugh. "Maybe not exactly a weirdo, but you have to admit, you're the one who always has the guys coming around."

"Not because of anything I do," Deanne tried to assure everyone. "It's probably just because they want discounts on surfboard rentals."

"Uh huh," Betty said with a wicked gleam in her eye. "I'm sure Jeff will be able to argue that point."

"Maybe she's right," Jeff retorted.

Everyone's heads snapped around, and they all glared at him. Betty spoke up. "I can't believe you just said that."

"No, it's true," he continued in his own defense. "By now I'm sure every single guy on campus knows that Deanne will eventually break his heart, so why set yourself up like that?"

"Is that how guys think?" Deanne asked him.

"Not on your life." Betty's voice came through

the titters. "Guys like to feel like they have something no one else can catch. Isn't that right, Jeff?"

He shrugged and smirked. "Well, yeah, sort of."

"See?" Betty had a smug grin on her face.

"But only until they mature and become men," he added.

"Give me a break." Betty wasn't about to let her brother get the last word in.

"It's true."

"And I suppose you consider yourself one of these mature men?"

He bobbed his head. "Now I am." He paused then added, "I'm now a responsible kind of man, not the heartbreaker people seem to think I used to be. I've grown up."

Betty rolled her eyes, causing everyone at the table to break into laughter. Leilani was laughing on the surface, but deep down she was wondering where all this was leading. Sure, she was immensely attracted to Jeff, but she wasn't about to let herself go over the edge for him, only to have her heart broken.

Jeff turned to Leilani. "Can you believe how nice I'm being and how cruel my sister is?"

Leilani wasn't sure what to say, so she just grinned and looked back and forth between Jeff and Betty. She wasn't about to get in the middle of this. However, she hoped to learn as much as she could—for future reference, of course. Besides, it was obvious that Betty was only kidding around, and she knew her brother could take it.

"Okay, enough about Jeff," Betty said. "I want to hear what's going on with all of you."

They each took turns telling Betty the latest. Leilani listened as Betty asked all the right questions. The others made comments that bordered on silly as each woman talked. When it was her turn, however, everyone listened seriously.

"A degree in business is an excellent choice for a woman," Betty said with approval.

Jeff nodded. "I agree. Companies have quotas to meet. Most of them have to hire a certain number of women."

Everyone groaned, and Betty tossed her napkin at him. "Leilani isn't a quota," Deanne said on her friend's behalf.

Rather than let others speak for her, Leilani spoke. "All I want to do is find a company that will let me get into a management training position and work my way up."

"Set your goals high, Lani," Betty advised as she cast a warning glance at her brother. "And don't let anything stand in the way of what you really want."

"Hey, let's lighten things up a little," Jeff suggested. "We're supposed to be having fun, not acting serious."

"I thought you were all grown up now. What's

wrong with serious talk?" Betty threw at him as she bent her head over the menu.

They each ordered one of the specialty seafood items and passed their plates around so everyone could try something different. It was one of the things Leilani loved about this group—they acted like they'd known each other all their lives and they shared everything. She felt warm inside as she realized how it felt to be part of a large family.

"Ready to get back to the castle?" Jeff asked.

Jeff held the door of the van for her, so she got back in the front seat. When their hands touched, she felt a spark of electricity shoot through her fingertips, up her arm, and then settle somewhere deep inside her. She quickly pulled her hand back. He closed the door gently but firmly.

As soon as they reached the house, everyone piled out of the van and went inside. Jeff tugged at Leilani's arm. "Take a little walk with me, Leilani?"

She tilted her head and looked at him curiously. "Me?"

He snickered. "Yes, you. That is, unless my sister scared you off."

"N-no, she didn't scare me. Why? Should I be scared?"

Jeff studied Leilani's face and slowly shook his head. "Maybe I should be the one who's scared."

Leilani stood there, stunned by his comment, not having any idea what to say next. Up until that moment, she'd only thought about her own attraction to Jeff. She hadn't given much thought to the notion that he might be just as attracted to her, and just as scared of his own feelings.

The two of them made it to the edge of the yard. Leilani wasn't sure if she should start walking or just stand there and see what Jeff was going to do.

He shoved his hands in his pockets and looked around, shuffling his feet. Leilani felt an overwhelming urge to comfort him. She took a tentative step forward, reached out, and touched his arm. He pulled back.

"Sorry," she said softly.

"No," he said without hesitation. "Come here, Lani."

Leilani grinned. "Only your sister calls me that."

"Is it okay if I do too?" Jeff swallowed so hard she could see his Adam's apple sink then rise again. "It sounds a little less formal."

With a soft smile, Leilani nodded. "Yes, that's fine."

Jeff pulled his hands from his pockets and took hers in his, pulling her toward him. "You're very pretty," he said.

"Thank you." Good thing they only had the light from the moon and streetlamps. She knew her dark skin was probably crimson right now, as hot as it felt from the inside.

"But what I like most is your sweetness and the way you're so soft-spoken."

"Really?" she said, looking up into his eyes.

"Really." He gently tilted her chin so she'd face him. "You speak few words, and they sound like the voice of an angel, yet you're obviously an intelligent woman who knows what she wants."

If he only knew how true his words were about knowing what she wanted, she thought. She swallowed hard as he stood there, gazing down at her, the subtle light enhancing the glow she felt encircling them.

Leilani knew he was about to kiss her. The electricity crackled in the space between them. She stood there, unable to take her eyes off his face, as he lowered himself to her. Just as their lips were about to touch, someone called from inside. "Lani, you out there?"

Jeff quickly pulled back. "I can't believe my sister." Turning, he called, "She'll be in when we're finished talking."

"Oh, Jeff, you're still here?"

"I'll be gone in a few minutes," he said.

"Take your time. I just wanted to make sure Lani was okay."

"She's with me."

Betty's laughter rang through the silence of the evening. "That's what I'm worried about. Seriously,

Lani, don't feel like you have to hurry. We'll go ahead and start the board game without you."

Leilani gazed up at Jeff and realized that he could have been with anyone he wanted. But he'd asked her to walk with him. That made her very happy.

The romantic department of her life had been one series of kiss-offs, coming from either her or whatever guy she liked. It had never mattered. Being with Jeff was different, though. *He* was different. She knew that if she allowed herself to fall for him, something in her would change forever. Was she ready for that?

Another thing she had to think about was the fact that she still had more than a semester of school left. Getting her college degree was very important to her. She'd be the first one in her family to earn one, and she knew it meant a lot to her parents. Not only that, she wanted to remain independent, falling in love only because she wanted to be with someone, not because she was financially tied to him. In this day and time, she knew that meant having a college degree.

"You do still want to go with me tomorrow, don't you?" Jeff asked as he gently squeezed her hands. She took the initiative and squeezed back. He smiled.

"Yes, of course I do," she said.

"We can take food and have a picnic. A party."

It didn't take her long to decide. She nodded and

said, "That sounds great, Jeff. Would you like for me to ask anyone else to come along?"

He sucked in a breath and slowly let it out. "Why? Do you want someone else with us?"

She licked her lips. Naturally, when he mentioned a party, she assumed he didn't want to be alone with her. Besides, would it be safe for her heart to be alone with him?

"I don't know," she finally replied. All she knew how to be was honest. She didn't know if she should be alone with Jeff right now at the risk of losing her heart to the wrong person, at the wrong time.

"Tell you what, Lani," he began. "If you want to go with me and let it be just the two of us, then that's fine. If you want to ask someone else to tag along, I don't mind that, either. It's up to you."

"But I thought you said we'd have a party," she said, wanting to get rid of the confusion between them. It was better to clear the air.

Jeff licked his bottom lip and offered a small grin. "Lani, we can have our own private little party. But it's your choice. A group, or just the two of us. Your call."

Man, did he make it difficult. Not only had he blind-sided her and attracted her like no one else ever had, he was being a total gentleman about it.

"I-I'd better go inside now. I don't want them to worry," Leilani finally said.

Jeff nodded. "I understand." But he didn't make a move. A conflicting tug had her wanting to run and at the same time hold onto him.

"C'mere, you."

Next thing she knew, Jeff had her in his arms, and he was kissing her forehead, then pulling back to look at her. Her arms dangled by her side for a moment before she decided she liked the feeling of this embrace. She slowly lifted her arms and wrapped them around his waist. He smiled down at her.

"Feels right, doesn't it?" he asked, never dropping his gaze from hers.

Leilani gulped and said, "Yes, it does."

"Then let's go with the feeling and see where it takes us."

That was what she really wanted for her heart, but her mind was sending off all kinds of alarms. What if she fell madly in love with him, and he left the island, never to come back? That was the biggest risk of all for a local Hawaiian girl who fell in love with a mainlander. But at this moment, she knew she was willing to take that risk. It felt too good to be with him. She had to see what would happen if she went with her feelings.

"Good night, my sweet Leilani," he said with tenderness.

As she pulled away from him, he grabbed her hand and held on just a little bit longer. Could she be dreaming, or was it as hard for him to let go as it was for her to leave?

"Good night, Jeff," she finally said before breaking away and running into the house.

Leilani felt all eyes on her as she opened the door and walked inside. She had no idea what to say. No one else spoke a word at first.

Betty saved the moment. "Want us to count you in? We're just getting started."

"Sure," Leilani said. "Give me a minute." She ran back to the bathroom to get a good look at herself before she exposed her feelings to her friends. Her mother had once told her that she was easy to read because her eyes were windows to her soul.

Finally satisfied that she could maintain some control over her emotions, Leilani emerged from the bathroom. She'd have to be careful not to look anyone in the eye for a few minutes, but she was okay now.

"Sure has been a long time since we had an all-night board game going," Betty said, not giving anyone else a chance to comment about Leilani's time alone with Jeff. Leilani was thankful for that.

Deanne burst into giggles. "Remember that time we had Jeff and a couple of his buddies over? We played teams."

"Yeah, and if I remember correctly, we beat the socks off the guys," Betty said.

Picking up her game money and counting it,

Deanne nodded. "Anthony didn't like us girls taking advantage of them like that."

Leilani instantly looked over at Betty to see her reaction. She knew that Betty had once been head-over-heels in love with Anthony, and she'd been devastated when they'd broken up. But right now, she looked cool as a cucumber.

"Most men don't like it when women beat them. But that's too bad, isn't it?" Betty said, acting unfazed by Deanne's comment.

"Are you making a statement, Betty?" Terri asked.

"Of course, she is," Deanne quipped. "Betty's always making a statement."

"I have no idea what you're talking about," Betty said, shaking her head. "I made a simple comment with nothing deep behind it."

"Oh, Betty, you got that wrong," Deanne said with a chuckle. "You're deep, even when you don't realize it. I used to be in awe of how you managed to get right to the nitty-gritty of things. If I was puzzled about something, all I had to do was come to you, and you'd solve my problems for me."

"I did?" Betty said, scrunching her nose. "And you actually listened to me? Scary world we live in when people start paying attention to the things I say."

"Yeah," Deanne agreed jokingly. "Very scary world."

Leilani sat back and enjoyed the light banter among her friends. This was what a large, loving family sounded like, she imagined. She'd always wanted that, and now she had it.

"Hey, Lani, what did you and my brother talk about out there for so long?" Betty asked as she turned to face her.

Everyone looked at Leilani, waiting for her answer.

Chapter Four

She thought she'd get away with remaining silent, but she should have known better. With a light shrug, Leilani forced a smile.

"We were talking about plans for his visit." That wasn't a lie. It just wasn't everything they talked about.

Betty lifted an eyebrow. "What sort of plans?"

This was one time Leilani wished her friend weren't so smart. Again, she shrugged. "Hanging out, a little bodysurfing, maybe even mudsliding, stuff like that. You know . . ."

Leilani held her breath as Betty continued to look at her for a few more seconds. She felt as if she had to pass some sort of test, and she didn't like how she'd gone from feeling like part of the family unit to being interrogated.

Betty turned to everyone else and pounded her flat palm on the table. "Mudsliding! I haven't done that in years! When are we going?" With a light chuckle, she added, "When I told my friends on the mainland that I actually used to get inside a cardboard box and slide down a hill of mud, into a natural pool of water, they thought I was nuts."

"Maybe you are nuts," Deanne said. "But then, aren't we all?"

Leilani blinked as she realized she'd been let off the hook. It was so fast, her head was still spinning.

"We thought we might go sometime later this week," Deanne continued. "That is, unless you have something else you'd rather do."

"I don't think so." Betty shook her head as she pondered a thought. "Let's see. Last time we went mudsliding, we came back with one broken arm, two pairs of ripped-to-shreds jeans, and totally trashed cars." She scooted her chair back and stood up. "Nope. Nothing I'd rather do than go mudsliding. I wouldn't miss it for the world."

"We thought so," Deanne said. "How about concerts? You up for that?"

"Anyone good gonna be here?" Betty asked.

Everyone shrugged and gave a different opinion. This group was diverse in its taste in music. Betty sat there and laughed as each person mentioned a musician who'd be at the park, and was met with groans and totally rude comments from the others. Leilani began to relax once again. The attention was off of her now, just the way she liked it. Growing up an only child had forced too much attention on her, and she did everything she could to redirect it when possible.

They sat up talking until the wee hours of the morning, when Betty finally made the announcement, "I've been up for a couple of days now. Time to hit the sack so I won't sleep the rest of the time I'm here."

"Me too," Deanne said as she stood and began to stack the money.

Leilani offered her bed to Betty again, but it was declined. "Maybe by the end of my visit," Betty said. "But now I can pretend to still be young and able to sleep on the floor."

As they settled in the room, Leilani knew she'd have a hard time falling asleep. She had too much on her mind. However, she didn't expect Betty to start another discussion about her brother.

"Lani?"

Leilani propped up on one elbow. "Yes?"

"Are you and Jeff going out while he's here?"

"Uh, yes." Were they really going out? "Well, sort of."

Betty smiled. "I can tell he's interested in you,

but don't think you have to take him up on his offers just to be nice."

Being nice was the last thing on Leilani's mind.
She wanted to be with Jeff. "Don't worry. I'll do
what I want to do."

"You sure?"

"Of course. Why would I do otherwise?"

Betty shifted on the futon to face Leilani, who
could see her friend's face clearly in the moonlight
that streamed through the window. "Because you're
about the sweetest young woman I've ever met. Jeff
can see it, too, and I think you've really got him
going."

"Really?" Leilani wasn't able to keep the hopeful
sound from her voice, in spite of trying hard to
sound neutral.

"Yes, really," Betty replied. "Jeff has always enjoyed being around women, as you well know, but
he's acting a little different around you."

"She's right," Deanne offered, startling both
women. Leilani had almost forgotten that Deanne
was in the room, and that she'd had a relationship
with Jeff once before. It would have been awkward
had it been anyone else.

"Sorry, Deanne," Betty said.

"No, really, you're right. Back when Jeff and I
were dating, he never once held back what he was
thinking. But he's acting a little different around
Leilani. Sort of quiet . . . contemplative."

"Subdued," Betty added.

"Yeah, that too." Silence fell over the room before Deanne spoke again. "I think Jeff might have grown up a little."

Betty's explosive laughter filled the room. "No way!"

"He's your brother. You're not being objective." Deanne had sat up to join the discussion, and Leilani once again found herself listening and taking it all in. "He seems much more grown up now, and . . . well, responsible."

"He's still the same old Jeff as far as I'm concerned," Betty argued.

"I've noticed a difference."

"Maybe," Betty admitted. "I s'pose you could be right. At any rate, he's definitely interested in Lani. Did you see the way he looked at her during dinner?"

"How could anyone miss it?" Deanne's eyes held an amused look. "Those sizzling glances were enough to melt an iceberg." She let out a long, audible sigh.

Leilani sighed, too, as quietly as she could. She was flattered beyond belief, but she wasn't so sure they were right. She needed to be careful too. If they were mistaken, she could wind up with a broken heart. And if they weren't, what would happen once the vacation was over and he had to head back to the mainland? Either way, she'd be hurt.

"Did Jeff say what he was doing today?" Betty asked. It was already morning, and they still hadn't been to sleep.

"We're going bodysurfing," Leilani answered softly.

"That's something my brother's really good at. But I bet you have a few things to show him."

"Let's try to get some sleep," Deanne said as she fluffed her pillow. "Tomorrow's already here, and I'm whipped."

Leilani lay there staring at the ceiling for a few minutes before she closed her eyes. Next thing she knew it was morning.

"I can't believe it's only nine, and I feel so rested," Deanne said as she hopped out of her bed.

Betty and Leilani were already up, pulling sheets up and folding the futon. Their room was on the eastern side of the house, so they had full sun beating down through the window.

"What time is Jeff picking you up?" Betty asked.

Leilani shrugged. "He's supposed to call me, but I think I'm driving." After all, he was visiting, and she had the car.

Betty tilted her head and arched one brow. "He's letting you drive?"

"Yes," Leilani answered, puzzled as to why this would raise suspicion. "What's wrong with that?"

"Oh, nothing, it's just that my brother likes to be in control. He rarely likes other people to drive."

Deanne turned to Leilani, snapping her fingers. "Last night, I heard him mention he was renting a car."

"I can drive."

"Not if I know him like I think I do," Deanne said, smiling.

Betty smiled and nodded. "I bet you're right."

"But it doesn't make sense," Leilani said, sitting down on the edge of the bed. "He doesn't have to spend money on a rental car."

"Lani, save yourself a lot of worry and don't even go there. Jeff can rent a car. He has plenty of money and nowhere to spend it. Let him do what he wants to do."

"But—"

"I know," Betty interrupted. "It doesn't make sense, but this is how he does things. Besides, he has a thriving business. Let him do this."

"If you're sure," Leilani said skeptically.

"I'm positive. Besides, if you try to talk him into letting you drive, he might discover he likes it, and then you'd always have to drive. This will save you a little gas, too."

"If you're sure, Betty," Leilani said slowly.

Betty reached out and touched Leilani's arm. "Look, Lani, I've known you a long time, and I know how sweet and wonderful you can be. But face it—you aren't all that experienced in the ways of men. My brother, on the other hand, has been around the block a few times. Take my advice on matters of the heart, especially when it comes to Jeff."

Leilani nodded. "Yeah, you're right."

"This is one time I know I am. Jeff is a sweetheart, and he's my brother and all, but I do know how hard it is to lose at the game of love."

Betty and Leilani looked at each other for a few seconds, a flood of understanding passing between them. Leilani had always looked up to Betty and taken all the advice her friend had been willing to offer. She needed to remember the wisdom she'd benefited from in the past.

"Okay, Betty. Thanks."

Deanne had already gone into the kitchen and started making toast. They generally had toast and bananas from the tree in their back yard when it was producing, which was most of the time. It was tasty and saved them money.

"There's nothing like breakfast at the castle," Betty said as she chomped down on the end of a banana.

"Very nutritious and delicious," Deanne said with a smile.

Leilani poured a cup of coffee and sat down at the table. She wasn't hungry yet, but she figured she could at least join her friends while they ate.

Betty turned to Deanne. "So tell me about your internship. When will you know something for sure?"

Deanne shrugged. "A couple of months, at least."

"Do you think you'll stay here after you get your Master's? Or will you be looking on the mainland?"

"I'll probably hang around here. But who knows? If the offer is good enough, I'll go anywhere."

Leilani took this opportunity to think about Jeff, since she knew all about Deanne's blueprint for the future. He was supposed to call her around noon to make plans for their trip to the beach. She decided she'd make an offer to drive, but if he really wanted to get a rental car, she wouldn't argue. It wasn't worth it, she figured. Besides, what did it matter? And Betty might be right.

"Hey, Lani, you with us?" Betty asked, shaking her from her personal thoughts.

"Yeah, I'm with you. I think I'll do a little work around here before Jeff calls," she said as she stood up. "This place gets messy fast."

"She's restless," Leilani heard Betty say as she left the room. "I've been that way when I've had to wait for a guy to call."

Leilani moved around the tiny house picking up things that were scattered on the furniture and floor. It only took about fifteen minutes, so she grabbed the feather duster and took a few swipes at all the surfaces. When she was finished dusting, she swept.

Less than an hour later, she was finished with everything in the house.

She'd noticed a few weeds around the outside of the house, so she decided to tackle them. The landlord sent someone over once a week to take care of the yard, but she needed something to do, or she'd go crazy. Leilani wasn't used to waiting for the phone to ring.

Finally, when she came back inside, she realized she needed a shower. "You're going to the beach," Marlene said. "You'll just get sandy and salty."

"I know," Leilani said, grabbing a towel from the linen closet in the hall. "But I'll feel better if I take a shower now."

Since she was going bodysurfing, Leilani knew better than to put on any makeup. It wouldn't last long; after the first wave, her face would be smudged. So she just applied a light touch of moisturizer.

Finally, Jeff called and Deanne answered. While she was chatting with Jeff, Betty stuck out her bottom lip and blew her bangs, causing them to fluff up in front. "It's about time he called. If he'd waited any longer, I'm afraid Lani would have started trying to clean *us* up. I've never seen this place looking so good."

Leilani picked up a pillow and tossed it at Betty good-naturedly as she moved toward the phone. "I just like it neat, that's all."

"Yeah, and waiting for my brother to call had nothing to do with it, right?"

Leilani shrugged. What was the point in denying it? Betty was right. Okay, so she was neat, but not usually to this degree. It had everything to do with Jeff.

They made plans for him to pick her up in about an hour. He quickly squelched any thoughts she had of driving. "Think you can be ready in an hour?" he asked. "If not, I can wait a little longer."

"No, I'll be ready," she said.

When she hung up, Betty playfully raised one eyebrow. "Why didn't you tell him you've been ready all morning?"

Leilani looked at her old friend. "Betty, how do you feel about me going out with Jeff? Does it bother you? Sometimes I think you're okay with it, but sometimes you act like it's not such a good idea."

Betty shifted her weight from one foot to the other, then she motioned for Leilani to follow her to the bedroom where they could have some privacy. Deanne had already gone to work, but Marlene and Terri were up and milling around.

As soon as they were in the room with the door closed Betty sat on the edge of Deanne's bed. Leilani sat on her own and said, "Okay, now tell me what you think about this."

Betty opened her mouth, then closed it before she

finally started talking. "As you have probably already figured out, my brother has never had trouble finding women who are attracted to him."

Leilani nodded. "Yes, I've known that for quite some time. Does that bother you?"

"No, of course not," Betty said with a throaty laugh. "In fact, I've managed to meet quite a few of my friends through Jeff. But I don't want to take a chance on losing a friend like you, either."

"Why would you lose me for a friend if I go out with him?" This confused Leilani. She'd never hold anything Jeff did against his sister, even if he hurt her.

Betty sighed. "I'm not saying this will happen, Lani, but if he ever breaks your heart, I'm afraid you'll transfer your feelings over to me. You and I have too good of a friendship for me to let that happen."

"But I wouldn't let it happen. If Jeff breaks my heart, I'll deal with it."

"You say that. But won't you feel awkward around me and unable to express your feelings, knowing I'll always be his sister?"

Leilani had to think about this for a moment. She hadn't thought that far ahead yet. "I can't see it being that bad," she finally said.

Betty stood up and placed her hand on Leilani's shoulder. "I have a long history with Jeff's ex-loves. He's broken many hearts, and I've been in all sorts of predicaments because of it, starting way back in junior high. I just don't want to lose you as a friend, and that's why I'm acting like I am. Nothing would make me happier than for you and Jeff to get together. That would be so much fun. But if the two of you ever had a falling out, I'd feel torn. Jeff is a wonderful brother and full of laughs, but you're special to me too."

"I promise to never put you in the middle," Leilani said after thinking about it. She saw it now. It could be a very difficult situation, and she didn't want Betty to feel torn.

"Promise something else."

Leilani cocked her head. "What's that?"

"Don't get so carried away with my brother that you lose sight of your dreams."

"If you're talking about school, that absolutely won't happen," Leilani said.

"In that case, go out with my brother and have the time of your life," Betty said, the tension easing from her face. "He's fun, and he's cute. Just remember what you promised. Our friendship will endure, no matter what my brother does."

"Don't worry so much," Leilani said. "I'll remember all my promises."

Leilani hung around the room after Betty left. She thought about everything they'd said, and she realized that there were some big differences between how Betty viewed things and her own perspective.

Leilani didn't see the conflict between love and personal ambition. Why couldn't she have both?

There might be some cultural differences, too, Leilani realized. She'd lived in Hawaii all her life, and people here accepted things as they happened without worrying so much all the time.

Betty and Jeff were from a small town in Arizona, where people knew and cared about one another. Jeff had mentioned that their family missed them, which was probably why they'd gone back home after graduation.

Over the years, Leilani knew that the roommates in this house had been an equal mix of locals and people from the mainland. But they'd blended well and learned quite a bit from one another.

It appeared to Leilani that Jeff actually considered himself more into the Hawaiian culture than Betty, although she'd fit in when she was here. Jeff had been the first of the two to go to the University of Hawaii because he'd earned a scholarship. Betty always thought it would be cool and adventurous to live on a tropical island, so she followed him a year later.

Something Leilani didn't want to have to do was worry about how to act around Jeff and Betty when they were all together. Hopefully, her fear of worrying her friend would vanish pretty soon. She didn't like the uneasy feeling in the pit of her stomach.

"He's here," Betty called. "My brother is used to waiting for his dates, so don't feel like you have to hurry."

"No," Leilani said. "I'm ready. He won't have to wait for me."

"Oh, I forgot," Betty said without the slightest hint of sarcasm, "you're one of those naturally beautiful women who doesn't have to spend hours in front of the mirror doing her makeup and hair."

"I probably should," Leilani said, feeling embarrassed by the matter-of-fact compliment.

"No, don't you dare. You're perfect as you are," Betty said in an admiring tone. "I can see why my brother can't take his eyes off you."

Yes, there was a physical attraction between her and Jeff. Leilani had to admit that was the first thing she'd noticed when they'd seen each other at the airport. But that wasn't all. She loved his quick wit and the way he seemed so at ease, no matter where he was. Hopefully, there was something beyond her physical appearance that he liked, too.

Jeff knocked on the screen door before Leilani heard Betty open the door to let him in. "She'll be out in a minute, Jeff. Did you remember to wear your sun block?"

The sound of his laughter reverberated through the house, warming Leilani from the inside out. "I swear, Betty, you sound like Mom. I don't need sun block."

"But you'll get burned," Betty argued.

Leilani smiled. It was nice hearing such loving words, one of the many things she figured she'd missed by growing up an only child.

She left her room, carefully closing the door so she wouldn't appear too anxious. But somehow, she couldn't keep the butterflies from fluttering around in her stomach.

Both Betty and Jeff turned and looked at her when she entered the living room, admiration apparent on their faces. "Wow," was all Jeff could manage.

Leilani had covered the bottom half of herself in a sarong, leaving the top half of her body covered only by her swimsuit. This was normal attire for Hawaii, but she now remembered that Jeff and Betty had been back on the mainland for a long time. She wished she'd chosen something else to wear.

She started to turn back to the bedroom to change, but Betty stepped forward and grabbed her arm. "Oh no you don't, Lani. You're perfect. Just make sure you have a towel, brush, and clip so you can show my brother a thing or two in the waves."

Jeff was grinning from ear to ear, obviously pleased with himself. "I used to be pretty good on the waves, but I'm probably a bit rusty."

Betty snorted. "Don't let him fool ya, Lani. He

taught everyone in this house but you how to body-surf. Jeff's good at any and all water sports."

"Why thank you, Betty," he said. "That's quite a compliment coming from you."

She shook her head. "Lani's still a better body-surfer than you, Jeff, and don't you forget it."

Chapter Five

As soon as they fastened their seatbelts, Jeff turned to Leilani. "So, you're a champion body-surfer, huh?"

She shrugged. "I wouldn't call myself a champion, but I do know my way around the waves."

"Good," he said, smiling as he backed out of the driveway. "It'll be fun to swim with someone who can keep up with me."

Just like that, he'd shown her that he was comfortable with her athletic ability. Most men had to prove their superiority, but not Jeff. It was one more point of proof that he was comfortable, no matter where he was.

Since half the day had already passed, they decided to go to the edge of Waikiki. "Next time we'll go to the North Shore, but I don't want to waste too much time driving."

Leilani nodded. She preferred bodysurfing at Sandy Beach, but Waikiki was fine. In fact, when she wanted to take a quick dip in the ocean, she generally hopped on the city bus and went to where they were going today. She knew the way the water broke there, and it would be fun, especially since she was with Jeff.

Jeff splashed and goofed around, making her laugh with his silly antics in the water. And after they caught the first wave, he praised her to the hilt.

"You have more control than anyone I've ever seen," he said admiringly. "And such finesse."

Grinning with pleasure and pride, Leilani said, "Thanks, Jeff. You're not so bad for a *haole* guy."

Jeff feigned a frown, and when she took a step closer to see if he was serious, he grabbed her, threw her over his shoulder, and carried her right back out to the water, where the waves were breaking. As he gently set her down in the waist-high water, she felt a shiver of excitement at his touch. He had a gentle but firm touch that caused an ache in the center of her chest. She wanted to hold onto him, but she couldn't see a graceful way of doing it.

He never took his eyes from her as she glanced over her shoulder to watch the wave that was fast approaching. "Ready?" she asked, wishing she could just stand there and hold onto him forever but knowing she couldn't. They were here to bodysurf.

"Ready," he said so softly she could barely hear him.

As if planned, choreographed, and rehearsed, they caught the wave together. And together they rode it to the shore, only standing up when the force of the water released them.

"That was incredible, Lani," he said as they surfed in together once again. "Not bad for a *haole*, huh?"

She nodded in agreement. Jeff was a wonderful athlete, handling the waves like he'd been born in them. Many people who'd surfed with her had been intimidated and tried things they weren't capable of, just to prove to her that they could keep up with her. She'd seen many guys bite the sand. In fact, she'd had to rescue the last *haole*, or mainlander, date she'd had. She thought it was funny; he never called again.

"Getting hungry?" Jeff asked.

At the question, Leilani's stomach started to growl. She smacked playfully at her flat stomach and nodded.

He grinned at her. "Let's grab something, then. How about some sushi?"

She raised an eyebrow. "You like seaweed and rice?"

"Love it," he answered as he took her hand and

pulled her to the beach, where they picked up their towels and dried off. Glancing up, he pointed to the vending trucks parked in the lot beside the beach. "Or if you want a *manapua*, I see they've got those too. I can't wait to have one. I told a friend who owns a restaurant in Arizona about the pork-filled dough, but he was never able to duplicate it."

"There are a lot of things here that can't be duplicated," Leilani agreed.

Jeff studied her with an approving gaze. "You can say that again."

Leilani gulped. Her knees nearly gave out, until he tugged on her and pulled her toward the food.

Since neither of them could decide what they wanted, and the offering was so great, Jeff stopped and bought one thing from each of the trucks. Then, he picked up two bottles of water and carried them to the blanket.

"Nothing like a feast filled with sand," he said.

After a couple of minutes, Leilani felt less self-conscious. The two of them ate heartily, devouring all the food.

"You sure can put down some chow," Jeff said enthusiastically. "Most women I know on the mainland eat like birds."

"Yeah, and they probably aren't trying to keep up with you in the waves, either," Leilani retorted. "That was quite a workout."

"Yeah, and much more natural than what you'd get at a gym," he added.

"I like to go to the gym." *And I like you*, Leilani added in her mind. She stopped chewing and studied Jeff.

He looked into her eyes, the moment suspended in time. Leilani felt as though the rest of the people on the beach suddenly didn't exist. It was just her and Jeff, the two of them sitting on the blanket, in a world that was far away from anything around them. She felt the hot intensity as his gaze raked her from head to toe. Then suddenly he shifted nervously.

They both looked away after a few more seconds. Jeff was the first to speak. "Is there anything you don't like to do?"

"Well," she said, "yeah. I don't like to hang out in bars."

"Neither do I," he agreed. "Too much smoke."

"Not to mention a bad environment for meeting people."

"That's true. No one acts normal in those places."

Leilani wondered if she was acting normal now. She suspected she wasn't. Her heart was beating double-time, in spite of the fact that they'd been out of the water for almost an hour. She had no excuse for her fast pulse, other than the fact that Jeff was sitting right there beside her.

"Wanna go for some more surfing, or do you need to get back?" he asked.

"Let's take a little walk on the beach while this food settles," she suggested. "I'd sink if I tried to ride a wave now."

Jeff hopped up to his feet, reached for her hands, and pulled her up beside him. He towered over her, making her feel small and fragile. Most of the time she forgot about her small stature, but with Jeff right there, holding onto her, she was very aware of every physical thing around them, and every single difference between them.

As they started walking, people turned and looked at them. Leilani knew it had to be because of the goofy expression on her face, but she couldn't disguise the way she felt. No matter what she did with her mouth, whether she smiled or talked, that same muscle twitched, and she knew she looked like a woman in love.

But how could she love Jeff? Sure, she'd known him for a couple of years. They hadn't been alone together very often. Most of the time, she'd been part of a group, and stood back watching him as he entertained everyone else.

Jeff was one of those people who kept people in stitches. He smiled easily, and he always saw the humor in every situation.

Jeff looked down at Lani and wondered how he'd gotten so lucky. He'd gone out with her a few times, but the warning from his sister kept him from pursuing anything beyond friendship. Betty had told him that Lani was a sweet girl who was focused on her education.

"She comes from a humble, middle-class family, and I think she wants to move up a notch," Betty had told him, and warned him to give Lani space. He never saw what one thing had to do with the other—whether he took her out on a date or not—but he did what his sister told him to do. He stayed away. Their mother's dropping out of college had more of an effect on Betty than it had him, probably because she thought their mother wasn't completely fulfilled. Jeff thought otherwise. If their mother had truly wanted to go back to college, she could have.

But now things were different. He and Betty were just visiting, although he knew there was a chance he might be moving back. Plus, Lani had a little more than a semester left of college, so she could branch out a little bit and start thinking beyond her studies now. At least that was what he hoped.

At any rate, he knew that Leilani Kahala was the most gorgeous woman he'd ever met in his life, both inside and outside. She was athletic, which suited him just fine. He loved the way she let go and followed through in her movements, something many women didn't do when they were around him. Her slender limbs were not only gorgeous, they were graceful, whether she was bodysurfing or just walking beside him. He even enjoyed watching her hands as she ate. Those long fingers had a sensuality of their very own, rendering him weak inside. But he sensed she was still holding back.

Jeff often wondered why women were so self-conscious around him when they first met him. He'd detected that a little bit in Lani, until they got in the water. Then, she really let loose and just rode each wave like a pro. And Betty was right. She *was* better than him. Much more graceful and fluid. She wore the water like a second skin, which gave him a rush of appreciation while he watched her. Lani's honey-colored skin glowed from the glistening droplets of ocean that beaded on her arms, neck, and face. Her dark hair was slicked back from her face, showing off her wide-set eyes and cute little nose. The white-ness of her teeth was enhanced by the deep copper color of her lips. Man, did he have it bad for this beautiful woman.

But Jeff was not only physically attracted to Lani, he also loved the way she thought. Her intelligence amazed him. She seemed to understand complex concepts, yet she never condescended to anyone who didn't. And she was quiet. She didn't seem to mind listening and waiting for others to speak their minds. Never once had he seen her vie for attention, be it his or anyone else's. She didn't need to. Just being her beautiful, thoughtful self brought her all the attention she needed.

Her sweetness touched his heart. Leilani was kind to everyone, smiling most of the time. Yet she was quiet and alert.

The idea of returning to Hawaii to live sounded better and better. Jeff knew he really needed to find work if he was serious about this. There were accounts here that shouldn't be too difficult to obtain. He should be able to maintain his largest account on the mainland and make periodic mainland trips to visit the company in person.

Although Jeff knew he was respected in business, his one big fault was his tendency to let things happen on their own. His "hang loose" attitude had actually helped him in the past, but now he knew he needed to become more aggressive to get what he wanted.

He missed the aloha spirit that permeated the islands. People on the mainland visited Hawaii and got a brief taste of it, but until a person actually lived here, they couldn't fully understand. Aloha spirit was that innate feeling he'd had from the moment Lani dropped the lei over his head, and it continued as they walked down the beach, relaxed yet happy beyond comprehension at the thought of a simple splash of a wave. It was the feeling he had inside when a local grinned at him, offered the "hang loose" hand gesture, and said, "howzit?" The fragrance of plumeria blossoms mixed with salt air was part of it, too. Pure magic seemed possible on the Islands.

"Jeff?" Lani said as she stopped and turned to face the water.

He quickly turned toward her. "Did you say something?"

"I was just thinking." She replied. So he hadn't been the only one. "Sally's flight will be here first thing in the morning, and I'm supposed to pick her up."

Jeff's eyes twinkled with humor. "Are you the taxi service?"

With a quick smile that gave him a shocking amount of pleasure, she nodded. "Apparently so, but I don't mind. It's kind of fun to meet people in at the airport."

"Yeah," he agreed. "I've always liked it. Especially here where I get to give them a lei and a kiss."

"Wanna come with me in the morning?" she asked, turning her head slightly away but still looking at him from the corner of her eye. It was a look she'd given him before.

Jeff nodded. "Absolutely. And I'd like to drive, too."

"That's not why I asked you, ya know."

"I realize that, but I want to."

"Do you know Sally?" Lani asked.

"Sally and I are old friends."

She snorted. "I should have known that. You're friends with everyone. I barely know her. She'd already graduated when I arrived, but she did occasionally come back for a visit. She worked in Honolulu for a couple of months before her company transferred her to the mainland."

"She's a pretty cool lady. Sally's the one who brought Betty to the castle."

In a sort of convoluted way, he could thank Sally for being here with Lani right now. If it weren't for Sally meeting Betty and inviting her to live in the house, he probably wouldn't even know Lani. Aloha spirit had something to do with this as well. Things that seemed to happen spontaneously in Hawaii were no accident, he was certain. And even though Sally wasn't one of his favorite people, he could tolerate her here.

As long as he was in Hawaii, he was willing to overlook some of the tension between him and Sally, especially if it meant he could spend more time with Lani. For reasons he never fully understood, Sally had a way of getting on his nerves. If he'd known her back in Arizona, he would have stayed as far away from her as he could get.

"Ready to go back now?" she asked as she turned to face him head on.

He wasn't, but he replied, "If you think we should."

"Marlene and Terri were supposed to buy some chicken and cook it on the grill."

Jeff wanted to be with Lani longer, but he wasn't about to invite himself to eat with the ladies. If they wanted him to join them, someone surely would have asked him by now.

All the way back to the house, he noticed little things that had changed since he'd been gone. He pointed them out to Lani.

"But nothing's really that different," Lani commented. "A few scenery changes, but deep down, this is still Hawaii, and the spirit of aloha is still the driving force here."

She'd read his mind. That was what he loved about this place. The spirit of aloha. It was something that couldn't be described in words, but anyone who'd spent any time at all on the islands knew what it was. It was feeling, an attitude, something in the air that went deep. It was everything he'd thought earlier and much, much more.

"What time should I pick you up in the morning?" he asked as he pulled into her driveway.

Lani started to tell him, but the sound of Betty's voice startled them. She was running from the house to the car. "I'm glad I caught you before you left, Jeff. Terri and I went shopping this afternoon for a cookout, and I bought enough chicken for you to join us."

Jeff felt his heart lighten. He wouldn't have to leave Leilani, after all. "You sure you don't mind?"

Betty rolled her eyes. "C'mon, Jeff, gimme a break. Do you think I'd waste my money on you if I minded?"

He smiled at Lani's giggle. "Okay. What time?"

Betty glanced at her watch. "You have time to take a shower and get back. Just don't dillydally."

Jeff shook his head. "You're starting to sound more and more like Mom."

She cast a look of mischief toward Lani, then turned back to Jeff. "Besides, you're cooking."

Lani's head whipped around to look at Betty. Jeff almost burst into laughter, it was so cute.

"Yep. Just like Mom."

Betty laughed. "Good. She's a smart woman."

Jeff got out and helped Lani get her things out of the backseat. Betty took the bag and towel and said, "I'll bring her stuff inside so the two of you can talk. Just remember what I said. We're eating in one hour."

Once Betty was inside, Jeff turned to Lani. "I had a nice time today. You're an incredible bodysurfer and an amazing swimmer."

"So are you," she said, looking up at him.

Her face was turned toward him just right, and he couldn't resist. He leaned down, reached out and tilted her chin a little bit more so he could see her better. After looking into her eyes, he dropped a kiss on her lips. When he pulled away, he saw the stunned expression on her face. He hoped it wasn't anything more than surprise. He wanted her to like the kiss as much as he had.

Leilani walked inside the house to face four pairs of eyes all focused on her. She smiled nervously.

"Did my brother behave?" Betty finally asked after a long uncomfortable moment.

With a quick nod, Leilani said, "Of course he behaved. What did you expect him to do?"

Deanne burst into a fit of giggles. "Should I tell her?"

Betty rolled her eyes, "Go ahead."

This time, when Leilani looked at Deanne, she saw a clouded expression. "Jeff is a very nice guy, but he's not the type to get serious about a woman, Leilani. He won't intentionally hurt you, but when he decides to go off on his own way, you'll wonder what in the world happened to you."

Betty nodded in agreement. "I have no doubt my brother likes you, Lani, but he does have a history of breaking hearts, although he's never mean."

Why were they telling her this? Was she that obvious?

"But maybe things are different now," Deanne added. "He's a little older, and time has a way of maturing people."

"Are you saying my big brother is immature?" Betty asked with a snicker. "I thought I was the only one who noticed." She glanced over at Leilani and added, "But like Deanne said, maybe he has grown up."

Leilani didn't know how to react. She just swallowed hard, shook inside, and said, "Jeff and I are just friends, that's all. We had fun bodysurfing and walking on the beach. Tomorrow he's going with me to pick up Sally."

Betty arched one brow. "Jeff's getting up at the crack of dawn to go with you to the airport? He must have it pretty bad for you, Lani, even worse than I thought."

"What do you mean?" Leilani asked.

"One of the reasons Jeff does better being self-employed is that he's a night owl. Definitely not a morning person. I might need to take back everything Deanne and I said if he's willing to get up early to be with you," Betty said, laughing.

"Oh, he's not doing it for me. He said he and Sally are old friends." Then, it dawned on Leilani that maybe Jeff and Sally had been more than friends. "Did they . . . ?"

Betty and Deanne both laughed. "No, not Jeff and Sally," Deanne said. "In fact, they got on each other's nerves so bad we had to keep them in separate rooms, even during parties."

"Really?" Leilani asked in disbelief. She couldn't imagine anyone being bothered by Jeff.

"It's really strange," Betty added, "because they're so much alike."

Leilani remembered very few details about Sally, but she knew she liked her. "Maybe that's it. I've heard that people who are just alike often clash."

"I'm really puzzled that Jeff wants to go with you to pick her up. I would have figured he would have tried to talk one of us into doing it so he could spend more time alone with you, if that's his reason," Deanne said.

"No, I think he might have something else in mind." Both Leilani and Deanne looked at Betty, who'd spoken. "Jeff is really working on some things. Maybe he wants to turn over a new leaf with people he hasn't gotten along with in the past."

"Very un-guy-like," Deanne said, making them all erupt in a fit of giggles. "I haven't met many men who actually care about things like that," she added when she caught her breath.

Leilani hadn't either. She knew that Jeff was special. But it still bothered her that she felt like she did, even knowing that he'd be gone soon. His relationship with Sally made her wary.

"I'd better go take my shower and get some of the sand and salt out of my hair," Leilani said as she headed toward the bathroom.

"Was Jeff able to keep up with you in the water?" Deanne called out.

"Of course, he was," Leilani replied. "He's a very good bodysurfer."

Her hair was tangled, in spite of the fact that she'd clipped it up on top of her head before going in the water. She'd bought a special strong clip for swimming, but her hair became so heavy when it got wet that it didn't stay up the whole time. She had to keep digging the barrette from beneath the tangled mess and redo it, each time, she was certain, making it look worse than the time before. Jeff had been enough of a gentleman not to say anything, though. After they'd gotten out of the water for the last time, she'd let her hair hang free, only brushing the surface so she wouldn't look like a used mop.

She had to dump half a bottle of detangler in her hair, but she finally got rid of the rat's nests. The shorts and tank top she'd chosen to wear were laid out on her bed, so all she had to do when she got to her room was change out of her robe and into her clothes. A light touch of lipstick was all the makeup she'd wear, since she wasn't into heavy globs of stuff that made her face itch.

By the time Leilani left her room, Jeff was already back. His hair was still wet from his shower, and he wore a pair of khaki shorts and a surfer T-shirt. She thought he looked really nice, very Hawaiian-casual. It was hard for Leilani to picture him in the three-piece business suit that was typically worn by the businessmen she'd seen from the mainland.

To her surprise and pleasure, Jeff already had a spatula in one hand and an oven mitt in the other. "They put me on outdoor kitchen duty the minute I walked in. I didn't have a chance to sit down," he explained with a grin. "Wanna join me on the lawn?"

She nervously nodded. "Sure."

It was impossible not to notice the curiously sly looks on everyone's faces. She knew she'd have to get used to that, living in a house with this many people. She'd had a few dates over, but never a roommate's brother. Her guests had usually left right away rather than hanging around and subjecting themselves to the suspicious gazes of her friends.

"You okay?" he asked as soon as they stepped outside.

"I'm fine. It's just that I'm not used to being watched so closely. Now I know how a goldfish feels."

Jeff snorted. "Better get used to it, Lani. My sister is ruthless, and she'll make sure everything goes like she thinks it should."

Leilani gasped. "I like Betty."

"I'm not saying anything bad about her. She means well. I love my sister, but she's got definite opinions about everything, including my love life and probably yours."

Love life? *Did he actually say that?* Leilani wondered. "I've never let other people's opinions affect me much," she said softly.

"I can see that, Lani," he whispered as he dropped the utensils on the table and turned toward her, taking her hands in his. "And that's one of the things I really like about you."

"It is?" She couldn't keep the hopeful sound from sliding into her voice. She wanted him to like everything about her.

Nodding, Jeff went on. "In case you haven't noticed, I've taken every opportunity I can find to be with you. Sometimes it might seem awkward, but I don't care. Betty can stare at us all day long, but it doesn't change the way I feel when I'm with you."

Leilani thought her heart would leap right out of her body. She felt the same way about Jeff.

"Is that why you're going with me in the morning to pick up Sally?" she asked, her voice tentative.

He looked like he was trying to suppress a smile. "Sounds like they told you about my strained relationship with Sally."

"Yes, they did," Leilani offered. "Do you dislike her?"

Jeff shrugged. "I like her just fine. It's just that we get on each other's nerves."

"Is it because you're so much alike?" she ventured.

"Did they tell you that?" This time he didn't hold back. He belted out a laugh. Then, he nodded. "I guess we are a lot alike."

"You don't have to go with me, you know," Leilani said. "I can pick her up, then we can do something later."

"No," he quickly replied. "I want to be with you every single minute possible. My time here is short, and I don't want to waste any of it."

Leilani knew he was about to kiss her again. It was written all over his face and shining in his eyes. She didn't resist when he pulled her to his chest and leaned down. Their noses touched. "Lani, I—"

He was interrupted by Betty calling from the kitchen. "Chicken almost done?"

"My sister's timing is amazing," he whispered to Leilani. Letting go of his tight grip but not taking his hands from hers, he hollered back, "Almost. Wanna come see?"

Betty took that as permission to step outside. She knowingly glanced back and forth between her brother and Leilani. "Smells good," she said. "Nothing like teriyaki chicken in Hawaii. The rest of the food is almost finished, so you two need to come inside when you get the chicken off the grill and onto the platter."

"Will do," Jeff said with a sigh.

"You did a nice job on that chicken," Leilani said as he carefully lifted each piece off the grill with tongs.

"That's my specialty," he quipped, waving another set of tongs around like a band conductor.

Leilani loved the feeling of this moment with Jeff. He had the ability to bring out happiness from deep inside her. She'd discovered feelings she never knew existed.

She'd been content most of her life, but the joy she felt with Jeff was exceptional, something that she knew could be addicting. Although she knew he was planning to return to the mainland, she couldn't keep her distance from Jeff. Occasionally, a thought flittered through her mind that she might need to be more careful, but one look from him made her melt.

And the look he was giving her right now was intoxicating. His arched eyebrow and the crooked smile on his face gave a comical cast to his handsome features. There was no way she'd be able to tear herself away from him.

"Ready to go inside?" he asked.

Leilani nodded as their gazes locked. Still standing almost a foot apart, Jeff lowered his face to hers, hovered for a second, then dropped a hint of a kiss on her nose. Her mouth went dry.

Chapter Six

Everyone was standing around the kitchen with plates in their hands. "It's about time the chicken was done," Deanne said. "I was ready to give up on it."

"Yeah," Betty agreed. "I'm starving."

Jeff feigned shock. "You can't rush the cook, ladies. I had to take my time to grill this meat to perfection."

Within minutes, everyone's plates were filled. "There's room at the table for all of us now," Betty said with authority. "But tomorrow, Jeff will have to find another place to eat."

"Is that any way to talk to the man who slaved over hot charcoal for you?" he asked as he cut a bite of chicken.

Leilani watched him lift the fork to his lips, mesmerized by how he made everything look so good. When his gaze met hers, she quickly looked down at her own plate and began to stab at the potatoes.

"Hey, this is the best teriyaki chicken I've ever tasted," Marlene said. "You'll have to give me your recipe."

Jeff shook his head. "Afraid I can't give it to you. It's an old family secret."

"My foot," Betty said. "All you have to do is slap the chicken on the hot grill and douse it with a bottle of teriyaki sauce." She laughed some more. "Besides, the chicken was already marinated."

Acting insulted, Jeff glared at her. "After generations of this recipe being passed down through the family and never revealed, you're letting them know our secret just like that?" He snapped his fingers for emphasis.

"You can't keep all the good stuff to yourself," Betty said as she stabbed at her chicken. "Mmm. This *is* good."

"That's because I have the right touch," Jeff quipped.

"I'm sure," Deanne teased. "I'll bet Leilani had something to do with it."

"Yes," he conceded, "she did. How can I go wrong when I've got the most gorgeous woman in the world standing beside me?"

Everyone dropped their forks and stared at Jeff.

He'd always been a charmer, but according to Betty, Leilani knew that he'd never compared any one woman to another. This had to be a first.

A slow smile spread Betty's lips. "Well, I'll be," she said.

"You'll be what?" Jeff asked, seemingly unaware that everyone else was staring holes through him in shock. He playfully raised and lowered his eyebrows. "I can think of a few things you might be."

Betty shook her head, still smiling, and replied, "This is a little different from what I thought."

"What?" he asked, carefully putting his fork down on his plate. "Why is everyone staring at me?"

Leilani knew, but she wasn't about to answer his question. She was terribly flattered by his comment, but she wasn't sure if he'd hurt anyone else's feelings, so she didn't even look at them. She moved her eyes from Jeff and focused on her plate.

"Don't worry about it, Jeff," Deanne finally said. "We're just trying to get used to the new you, that's all."

"New me?" he asked as he picked up his fork. "Now what's that supposed to mean?"

"Oh, nothing," Marlene offered, looking conspiratorially between Betty and Deanne. "Terri, would you please pass the cole slaw?"

The conversation moved from the subject of Jeff to Sally's arrival the next morning. "I thought we'd try mudsliding after she got here. Remember last time we all went, and Sally got wedged between those two trees?"

This started a whole new line of discussion and laughter. Leilani only halfway listened to them as her thoughts wandered back to what she'd do once Jeff left the island. She already knew she'd miss him. It wouldn't be easy, but she didn't want to think about it now.

After dinner, Jeff was the first one at the kitchen sink, filling it with water and detergent. "I'll wash, you dry," he told Betty.

"Wait a minute," Deanne pouted. "I want to have some fun too."

"You rinse," he ordered.

Leilani watched as everything fell into place with Jeff at the helm. He was a very organized, take-charge kind of person. He never once acted uncomfortable about being the only man in the group. In fact, he didn't even seem to have preconceived ideas of what the others should and shouldn't do because of gender. He'd cooked, and now he was cleaning. What a great guy! Maybe he wasn't perfect, but Leilani liked everything she saw, with one exception. She needed to accept that he did have a love-em-and-leave-em reputation. Even if he'd matured and gotten past wanting variety, he was only here for a visit. She still thought he was an incredible man.

No way could he be perfect anyway, Leilani told herself as she finished putting plastic wrap on the salad. In fact, Jeff couldn't be half as good as he seemed. She was certain that if she watched him long enough, she was bound to see some major flaw that would bother her more than his reputation did. Besides, watching him would be fun—an exercise in human nature. Watch the guy and wait for the fall. Maybe, just maybe, she'd find a reason to be glad when he left.

A few minutes after they finished cleaning the kitchen, Jeff motioned for Leilani to follow him outside. "I can't hang around here very long. Betty gave me the signal it was time to leave."

Leilani hadn't seen this, but she didn't say anything. She just stood there and listened as Jeff continued.

"And since I have to get up at the crack of dawn, I'd better head on out."

"You don't have to go with me, you know," Leilani said, giving him another opportunity to back out if he wanted to.

"I really want to go tomorrow morning," he said firmly, casting a sideways glance back toward the house. Then, without warning, he leveled his gaze on her, weakening her knees. "That is, unless you don't want me to."

"Oh, that's not it," she said with a nervous laugh. "I do want you to go. It's just that—"

Jeff reached out and lightly touched his fingers to her lips, shushing her. "I'm going, and that's final. I'll pick you up at six-thirty."

Leilani nodded. He leaned forward and kissed the tip of her nose before he took a step back and got into his car. "See you in the morning," he said as he backed out of the driveway.

She stood there and watched as his car slowly drove up the street, away from her, taking part of her joy with it. "It's not that bad," a voice said from behind her, causing her to jump. "Sorry," Betty said. "Didn't mean to scare you. I wanted to make sure everything was okay."

Leilani sighed. She didn't mean for it to be as loud as it was, and there was no way to take it back. "I'm not used to feeling this way," she finally admitted.

"Never been in love before?" Betty asked in her understanding tone.

"No," Leilani said. "Never. Have you?"

"Once."

"With Anthony?" Leilani asked as the two of them headed slowly back to the house.

"Yes, but don't you dare tell anyone." Betty was kicking the ground as she walked, making little marks in the dirt. "How did you know?"

Leilani shrugged. "I just sort of figured it out. Did it hurt when he broke up with you?"

Betty stopped and sucked in a deep breath, and slowly let it out. "He didn't break up with me."

"He didn't?" Leilani was confused. "What happened?"

With a shrug, Betty resumed walking. "I figured that since I was going to graduate and probably find a job on the mainland, I might as well break it off before we got too involved."

"Surely you could've worked something out."

"I didn't think so at the time. Anthony was determined to remain in Hawaii, regardless of where his career led. I wanted to be an upwardly mobile professional. Our ambitions clashed."

"I understand," Leilani said. "That's what I'm worried about with Jeff."

"Me too," Betty admitted. "I don't want you to make any mistakes, Lani."

Leilani blinked. "What kind of mistakes?"

"Don't jeopardize your future."

"Oh, I have no intention of doing that."

"He really likes you, Lani," Betty said.

Something in the way she sounded made Leilani look at her friend. "What makes you say that?"

"I can tell by the way he looks at you and the way he refers to you as the best and prettiest of everything." Betty laughed out loud. "He's always been so careful before, never to compare any of his girlfriends to each other—especially in front of a bunch of women. He was probably afraid he might ruin a future opportunity. Now he doesn't seem to care."

That simple comment made Leilani's heart flutter. "I'm sure he realizes our relationship can't go anywhere with him on the mainland and me here."

"What if he moves back?" Betty asked, stopping again about three feet from the porch steps.

"Is there any chance of that?" Leilani asked, feeling hopeful.

"Who knows?" Betty took that last step before going inside. "When you're in love, anything's possible. Just wait until you graduate before you get too involved, though. Love can be blinding."

Whoever said anything about love? Leilani wondered. Sure, she felt some sort of infatuation, but she'd only been with Jeff for a few days. Though, there were times she thought she might be falling in love. And yes, she'd known him before, but not like this.

Leilani was so confused now, she didn't want to think about it anymore. She went inside and suggested a quick board game hoping to get her mind off Jeff. It wasn't long before all five women were sitting around the table playing and laughing over some of the silliest words they could think of.

Morning came quickly. The game was so much fun, Leilani hadn't gotten to sleep until way past midnight. And when her alarm clock sounded, she thought she was dreaming.

"Are you gonna shut that thing off?" Betty mumbled. "Or do I have to kill it?"

Leilani stood up, hit the clock with her palm, and stretched. She padded to the bathroom, took a shower, and dressed as quietly as she could. She barely had enough time for a cup of coffee before Jeff was due to arrive to take her to the airport to pick up Sally. Why Sally chose to fly through the night on a red-eye was beyond her.

When Leilani stepped outside it was still partly dark. The sun was barely peeking over the tops of the houses across the street. Most of the time this was her favorite time of day, but not this morning. She was exhausted.

She heard Jeff's car as it rounded the corner. He pulled into her driveway at exactly 6:30.

Glancing at his watch, he grinned. "Right on time and at your service, ma'am."

"*Mahalo*," she said.

"You're welcome," he replied, looking at her curiously before putting the car in reverse.

"What?" she asked, wondering out loud why he'd looked at her like that.

Jeff shook his head. "I'm amazed at how beautiful you are first thing in the morning."

Leilani smiled. She couldn't help it. Jeff had a way of making her feel so special, and she wasn't capable of acting cool and aloof, no matter how hard she tried. She loved the way he gazed at her and complimented her. She remembered what Betty had said about him acting out of character by comparing her to others.

"I hope Sally's flight is on time," she said, to make conversation.

"Most early morning flights generally are," he replied. "Sally always did have odd timing."

Leilani laughed. "Don't forget, I've heard that you and she are a lot alike."

"My sister won't let me forget that." They stopped at a traffic light, and he looked at her, turning her insides to mush. When the light turned green, he accelerated. "But I think she's nuts."

"Maybe," Leilani said. "I'll let you know."

Sally chattered nonstop from the moment she arrived to when they pulled up to the house. Jeff was mostly silent, which confused Leilani because she'd halfway expected to act as referee.

Betty and Deanne had woken up and were waiting for them when they pulled in the driveway. Jeff reached out and took her arm when she opened the car door.

"Can you spare a minute for me?" he asked, his voice cracking.

"Uh, sure," she said after looking to make sure Sally's things were all out of the car. "Just give me a couple seconds."

Leilani went up to Betty, who was watching Deanne help Sally. "Jeff asked if I could talk for a minute before he leaves."

"He's leaving?" Betty asked, a surprised expression on her face. "Tell him he should at least come in for coffee."

"Okay," Leilani said. Then, she went back to Jeff and watched while the other women went inside.

"Lani," he said softly, gently pulling her to him. "How was I?"

"Wh-what do you mean?" she asked, breathless.

She looked at him and noticed the strain that was evident in his eyes. "I kept my mouth shut," he said. "I was afraid I might start something if I opened it."

"Oh," Leilani said, suddenly understanding why he'd been so quiet on the way home. "That bad, huh?"

He folded his arms across his chest and pursed his lips in a tight, forced grin before agreeing. "Afraid so."

So now she'd seen a major weakness in Jeff. Still, she felt that incredible attraction to him.

Leilani sucked in a breath and let it out. "Betty said to ask you in for coffee."

"What would you like me to do?" he asked, studying her intently.

"The question is: What would you like to do?"

She wasn't about to make his decisions for him, no matter how he felt.

"Honestly?" He waited for her to nod before continuing. "I really don't want to go inside right now. I need to recover first. I'd almost forgotten how badly she gets on my nerves."

"Wow!" Leilani said. "I had no idea it was so bad. I appreciate you not arguing with her, although I can't imagine what you would have argued over."

"I'm sure we would have found something if I'd opened my mouth."

"In that case, I'm glad you didn't."

Jeff backed away and placed his hand on the car door. "I guess we're more alike than I care to admit. Let me run back to Anthony's house and grab something to eat. I'll call you later."

"Okay." Leilani watched while he drove away, feeling like a piece of her heart went with him again. Why did she feel this way, after only a few days? It wasn't fair to have something like this happen, knowing that it would be taken away in a very short time.

"Where's Jeff?" Sally asked when she went back inside.

Leilani shrugged. "He had a few things to do, so he left."

Sally started to say something, but she quickly shook her head and clamped her mouth shut. Betty came forward and whispered, "It's probably for the best."

Leilani nodded.

While the women stood around and caught up on old times, Leilani saw Betty watching her from the other side of the room. There was a curious expression on her face, and she knew they'd talk later. Betty was good about that. She had a memory that wouldn't quit, but she always had great timing.

"So, when are we going mudsliding?" Sally asked.

"How's tomorrow?" Deanne said.

With an amused twinkle in her eye, Sally said, "You don't waste any time, do you?"

"We don't have time to waste," Deanne replied. "I hope you brought jeans."

"I did."

"Are you going?"

"Wouldn't miss it for the world."

"I'm surprised you're not afraid to slide after what happened to you last time," Betty chimed in. "In fact, I'm starting to think I'm too old for this kind of horseplay."

Everyone groaned. Betty wasn't the oldest one in the group; Sally was. But she was by far the most sensible one.

"C'mon, Betty, you're not getting out of it now." Deanne had her hands on her hips and was speaking with authority.

Betty held up her hands in surrender. "Don't worry. I don't want to be the party pooper. I'll go."

Sally had some coffee, then went to Marlene and Terri's room to put her things away. The house was as full as it could get. If anyone else wanted to stay there they'd have to sleep on the sofa, and the one they had was too small for most people.

Betty took advantage of the little reunion to talk to Leilani in private. "How was my brother on the ride home?"

"He was good, but quiet."

"I figured that. Are you upset with him for some reason?"

"No," Leilani replied. "But I have to admit, I am still confused. If he's so much like Sally, then why do they have so much trouble getting along?"

"Really want to know?" Betty asked with one eyebrow raised and a look of warning in her eyes.

Leilani's heart sank. "I think so."

"Okay, let's go for a walk around the block. I'll tell you everything."

As soon as they left the house, Betty began the story of how Sally had brought a guy to the castle whom Jeff didn't like. He'd called the guy a player and warned her to stay away from him. Sally became defensive and told him to mind his own business. She'd even told him he was the pot calling the kettle black.

"Then, when this guy started two-timing her and

treating her like she didn't matter anymore, Jeff suddenly became a know-it-all and said 'I told you so.' No one likes that."

Leilani agreed. "But why did that cause such a long-standing problem between them? It seems like they'd both be over it by now."

"Well," Betty began, "Sally's pretty strong-willed. Jeff didn't stop at that. He continued to scrutinize the men she went out with, and he always found something wrong with them."

"Was it because he had a thing for her?" Leilani ventured a guess.

"He might have at one time. But I think at this point it was more of a matter of clashing ego. She wanted to pick her own guys, and he wanted her to listen to him. He had a point to prove." Betty paused for a moment before adding, "I have a feeling that if she'd admitted to him that he was right that first time, he would have backed off."

"Why do you think he was so quiet in the car on the way from the airport?" Leilani asked.

"Probably because every time he voices an opinion, Sally nearly takes his head off." Betty looked amused. "And both of them have very strong opinions about everything."

Leilani did remember how Sally had chattered incessantly. And when she'd glanced over at Jeff, his jaw was clenched like he was grinding his teeth. Now that she thought about it, she wanted to laugh.

"Should I tell Jeff not to come mudsliding with us tomorrow?" Leilani asked, feeling really torn between Sally and the man she wanted to be with.

"Of course not," Betty said. "But it would probably be best if we went in two separate cars and kept them as far apart as possible."

Chapter Seven

Since Leiliani had a car, she drove. Betty drove Jeff's rental car, and Sally and Terri rode with her. Jeff, Marlene, and Deanne rode with Leilani.

"I hope we have enough cardboard boxes. Last time we each went through three," Marlene said.

"If I go through three boxes, I'll be ready to quit," Jeff stated flatly. "I'm not even sure I can still do this."

"Oh, come on, Jeff," Deanne teased. "You're the one who talked us into going the first time."

"Yeah," he said. "That was back when I was a foolish college student. I'm a responsible adult now." He made a face.

Both Marlene and Deanne snorted through their

noses. Even Leilani had to laugh, Jeff was being so comical.

The drive was fun, and it seemed like it took them no time to get to their favorite spot in the forest. There was a small clearing off the road, where no one would see them. They parked their cars, each grabbed a box from the back of Jeff's rental car, and started hiking up the side of the mountain.

"Hey, Sally," Deanne called. "Watch for those trees. If you see two of them standing close together, try to slide the other way."

"Don't worry about me," Sally responded. "I've already had that experience. It's the rest of you I'm worried about. Especially Jeff."

Everyone's head snapped around to see Jeff's reaction. He just waved. "I'll be fine."

Betty's eyes widened. "What did you do with Jeff, Lani?" she asked. "Because I'd know my brother anywhere, and that can't be him."

Leilani was puzzled too. Although she'd never been around Jeff and Sally together, she agreed that he wasn't acting like himself today—he was much more restrained, and not at all relaxed.

I'm going to keep my mouth shut if it kills me, Jeff thought. Getting into a battle of wills with Sally wouldn't do anyone a bit of good.

As Jeff hiked behind the women, he had to bite his tongue more than once. It seemed like he was the only one doing it, though. Each time she opened her mouth, he knew he could best her, but what purpose would that serve? The only thing he could think was that his reaction might reveal a negative side of him, and he didn't want that.

When they got to the top of the mountain, they all stood there and looked down. Jeff felt a rush of adrenaline bolt through his body. This was really living. He was glad he'd been talked into going mudsliding again. Being in business on the mainland seemed to have drained him of joy. But having spent a few days in Hawaii, he knew he wanted to come back as soon as possible. He hoped at least one of his business deals would come through. If not, he'd have to figure out another way.

"Ready?" he said as he put his box down and tested the slickness of the mud.

Sally threw her box in front of him and jumped on top of it. "Last one down is a rotten egg."

Jeff waited a few seconds, then followed her down. Everyone else slid behind him, waiting long enough so they wouldn't run into each other.

At the bottom of the steep slope, there was a small spring with clear water for them to take a quick dip before heading back up and starting the slide all over again.

Leilani managed to keep up with the rest of them, and Jeff noticed she was the only graceful one of the lot. Her slender frame was as strong as the rest of them, and she was more agile than everyone else. Jeff had a hard time not staring in amazement at her graceful beauty.

They slid and splashed for several hours before Jeff finally figured they'd had enough. "We need to get as much of this mud off us as possible," he said. "I'd hate to mess the cars up too much."

Leilani looked at him with a wistfulness he couldn't comprehend. Man, was she gorgeous!

As the day wore on, Leilani found herself falling, not only down the mountain in her box, but for Jeff as well. Was this love? *How could it be?* she questioned. If not, it was something pretty close, she imagined.

Jeff managed to have fun while being a gentleman and looking after the rest of them as if he'd been put in charge. The only one who didn't seem to appreciate it was Sally, and now Leilani saw what everyone else was talking about.

Sally was, indeed, very much like Jeff. Her nature was to be in control, and after being with Jeff, she'd seen that trait in him too. However, there was one big difference. Sally was used to being the life of the party, but no matter what she did, Jeff managed to upstage her. Sally pouted a few times, but she quickly recovered. Still, she always spoke her mind, Leilani noticed.

Once, when Jeff made a comment, Sally argued

with him. He opened his mouth, glanced at Leilani, then closed his mouth and forced a smile.

Was he doing this for her sake? If so, he didn't need to. Leilani could handle their bickering. Jeff didn't have to be on his best behavior for her. Betty had told her how Jeff and Sally were almost like brother and sister sometimes.

At the end of the sliding, Jeff suggested going home. Sally glared at him for a moment before she put her hands on her hips and said, "I want to slide one more time." It looked to Leilani like Sally was daring Jeff to argue with her. He didn't.

Sally and Terri went up the side of the mountain while the rest of them stayed in the water at the bottom. There was mud caked on the back sides of their jeans, and Leilani didn't want it all over her car. Water was okay, but not all this dark grayish-brown mud.

"Hey, why don't I take Marlene and Deanne back so Jeff and Leilani can have a little time alone?" Betty asked.

Sally squinted her eyes, glanced at Leilani, and finally said, "Okay, good idea."

They agreed to meet back at the house. It took a few minutes to get all the boxes broken down and into the back of the car, on top of the plastic Jeff had brought. Betty's group left first. Leilani and Jeff followed close behind.

Leilani pulled back onto the road. She could feel

Jeff looking at her, but she focused on her driving. When he reached out and touched her cheek, she flinched instinctively. He pulled his hand back.

"Sorry," he said. "I couldn't resist."

She licked her lips. "That's okay. It feels nice when you touch me."

"Are you sure?" he asked as he rested his hand on her neck.

Leilani had to swallow before she could talk. Each time she was with Jeff she felt something strong building up inside the pit of her stomach. She wanted to spend more time with him, but she was constantly reminded of what she'd have to deal with once he was gone. As haunting as that thought was, she still longed for more of him.

"I had fun today," he said softly.

"So did I." She pulled up to a stop sign, looked both ways, then pulled out. Each movement of her foot on the pedals seemed to take more energy than usual.

"What are you doing tomorrow?" he asked.

Leilani offered him a quick glance before returning her attention to the road. "I'm not sure. Sally said there were a few things she wanted to do while she was here. I don't know if she wants everyone to be with her or if she's got other ideas."

"Don't let her tell you what to do, Lani," Jeff said.

Leilani quickly snapped her attention to him and

frowned. She felt her first hint of anger toward Jeff. "That's not what I'm doing, Jeff. Sally is one of our old roommates, and this is supposed to be a reunion. We decided before she and Betty arrived that we'd do whatever the mainland roommates wanted to do, since we still live here." She felt defensive about her friends.

Jeff tilted his head forward and then turned to her apologetically. "I'm sorry, Lani. It's just that I want to spend every waking moment with you."

All the fight left her body the instant he said that. "Don't apologize, Jeff," she replied. "I'm flattered you feel that way. It's just that we're old friends, and we want to hang out together. That was the purpose of this whole thing."

"I know," he said.

Leilani reached out with her right hand and gently patted his leg. "I want to be with you too, Jeff."

When she pulled her hand back she felt him looking at her. The sizzling sensation inside her was so intense she had to widen her eyes to keep her mind on her driving. Jeff had already caused her enough mental anguish. She was forever worrying and being reminded of his imminent return to the mainland, so why did she keep seeing him? She knew the answer to that question the moment she asked herself. There was no way she'd be able to turn down an opportunity to spend time with this wonderful man sitting beside her.

When they got to the house, Betty was outside waiting for them. She smiled at Leilani and said, "I need a minute to chat with my brother. We won't be long."

Leilani nodded and headed toward the house. She'd try to jump in the shower befre anyone else did, since she seemed to be the one who could get ready the fastest.

While the rest of the women were in the kitchen, still standing to keep from getting the furniture wet, she showered, dried off, and changed into shorts. Betty and Jeff were still outside talking when she glanced out the window.

"Got it bad, huh?" She was startled by a voice behind her. When she glanced over her shoulder, she saw that it was Sally.

Knowing there was no use in denying her feelings, she said, "I s'pose."

"I understand," Sally said.

Leilani turned and faced her old friend, the only roommate she didn't know very well. "You do?" she asked.

Sally grimaced, then laughed. "I know it seems like I don't like Jeff, but I really do. It's just that . . ." Her voice trailed off as she tried to find the right words.

"You're so much alike?" Leilani offered, finishing Sally's sentence for her.

"Yeah, that's right. Betty kept trying to tell me

that, but I never saw it until today. I was watching Jeff, and I knew she was right. He and I both are very opinionated, and we speak our minds."

"He didn't say too much today," Leilani countered.

Sally let out a breath. "That's what made me realize she was right. I noticed how he held back, probably because he didn't want to upset you."

"Really?" Leilani asked. "You think that's why he was so quiet today?"

"I think so. I tend to do the same thing when I'm around a guy I want to impress."

Leilani wanted to hug Sally. But she just nodded and turned back to the window again.

"Did you know that Betty is thinking about moving back?" Sally asked.

"I know she'd like to."

"She's already asked for a transfer with her bank. In fact, she talked to me about doing the same thing."

"Is it possible?" Leilani asked, excited.

Sally shrugged. "Anything's possible, but it's highly unlikely that my company will let me move here. They really need me in my office."

"Maybe you can come back someday," Leilani said as she thought about how fortunate she was not to have that problem yet. She hoped she'd be able to live anywhere she wanted to live after graduation.

"Maybe." Sally now stood at the window right beside Leilani. "He's really a good guy."

"Jeff?"

"Who else? It's just that the chemistry between us has always been a little explosive."

"Yeah, I know what you mean."

Sally laughed out loud, then stopped and looked at Leilani. "It's definitely explosive between you and him too, but in a good way."

"I'm not so sure it's all good," Leilani stated sadly. "He's going back, and I'm still here."

"That can change, you know."

"I know," Leilani agreed, "but I still have a few months of classes. After that, who knows?"

"Yeah," Sally said with a sigh. "Who knows?"

Betty came back inside and made the announcement that it was time to plan the big party. "I was hoping we could do it next week, but Jeff has some business to attend to. He's worried that he might have to fly back this weekend."

Leilani's heart fell with a huge thud. *There goes any hope of future happiness together*, she thought.

She sat and listened as the rest of the women discussed who they needed to call and what kind of food to serve. "We should probably reserve a cabana at the beach," Deanne said. "That way we won't have to worry about space and parking."

"Sounds good," Betty said. "Why don't you check into it, Deanne?"

Sally drummed her fingers on the table. "I'll take care of the food. We can cook some here, and I'll take up a collection to get some munchies for the snack table."

"Munchies?" Deanne said, giggling. "Remember, we're in Hawaii, and we call them *puupuus*."

"Yeah," Sally said with mock sarcasm. "Try that on the mainland. People will think you've flipped. I learned that the hard way. I call them munchies now. At least you know what I'm talking about."

Betty turned to Leilani. "Are you okay with this, Lani?"

"Of course," she replied. "Why wouldn't I be?"

"I don't know, you just look so distraught." Betty narrowed her gaze and studied Leilani.

"I'm fine. Don't worry about me. And I'll bring the sushi. My uncle still has his deli, and he makes it fresh everyday. Maybe he'll take pity on us poor college students and make a donation to the cause."

Betty smiled and nodded. "That's right Lani, use your charm."

"Goodness knows," Sally said. "She has more than her share of charm."

Leilani wasn't sure how it happened, but Betty slowly lost control of the plans to Sally. By the time the discussion was over, Sally was issuing orders and telling everyone what was expected of them.

"Did you see that?" Deanne said after Sally had left the kitchen. "Sally is so good at delegating."

"Yes, she is," Betty agreed. "But she took a little longer to do it this time. I kept giving her opportunities to jump in and take over, but she waited so long, I didn't think she'd ever do it."

"People do change, you know," Deanne said. "In fact, I was amazed at Jeff's self-restraint today in the mud. Never, and I mean never, would he have let Sally get away with talking so much in the past. He was amazingly calm."

"Yes, he was," Betty agreed. "But I'm sure he had a valid reason for holding back."

Deanne beamed at Leilani. "Yes, I'm sure he did."

Betty sighed. "My brother and Sally aren't the only ones who are changing. I'm starting to mellow out a bit myself."

"You?" Deanne shrieked. "Mellow? Never!"

"Oh yes," Betty argued. "I don't feel as crazy as I once felt. In fact, I'm starting to worry that this party will get out of hand."

"Oh no!" Deanne said, slapping her forehead. "You've gone and matured on us."

With a glint of amusement in her eyes, Betty said, "Afraid so, my friends. Afraid so."

Leilani thoroughly enjoyed the playful discussions this group had. She certainly laughed a lot. She'd never been a big talker, but she was no shrinking violet, either. She spoke when she had something important to say.

"Jeff said he might have to leave early, depending on when his flight takes off," Betty said.

"Does he have to?" Leilani asked before she could stop herself.

Betty offered her a sympathetic look. "He doesn't have a choice, Lani. His business is very demanding. I thought you understood that." She hesitated a few seconds before adding, "One of his accounts is giving him some resistance about working from Hawaii. In fact, it may not work out."

Leilani looked down at the table. It took everything she had not to burst into tears. She had to bite her bottom lip to keep the tears from falling from behind her lashes, but she managed to compose herself, although she couldn't speak.

Deanne reached over and touched her arm. "I'm sure he'll be back."

"Of course he will," Betty agreed. "No way will Jeff be able to stay away forever from the place he loves."

Leilani didn't want to hear all about how Jeff probably planned to visit Hawaii. She'd hoped he'd find a way to stay so they could be closer to each other and find out where their relationship could go. Obviously, that wasn't the way it was going to be, so she might as well toughen up and get used to that idea.

After they went to bed, Leilani lay there with her eyes wide open. She ached inside. The only man she'd ever felt this way about was going to leave after the party tomorrow night, and she might never see him again.

Morning came, bringing noisy, cheerful birds and a houseful of roommates and ex-roommates who smiled more than Leilani felt like smiling back. She wanted to run and hide, at least until the party was over. How would she be able to face Jeff, knowing that he put his business before her feelings?

The phone rang off the hook all day with people accepting invitations. Somehow, Sally had managed to find a ukulele band to entertain, promising them a good time. Leilani went to see her uncle, who promised to have a platter of sushi ready an hour before the party. Everything was going just great, except her heart felt like it would break in two.

Jeff had called, but unfortunately, Leilani wasn't there to take the call. Betty relayed the information to her.

"He said he'd meet you there. He's picking up a couple of his old friends, and he asked if we could take them back to their apartment later. I told him I didn't think you'd mind."

"No, of course not," Leilani said. "I don't mind taking anyone home." She felt numb, so what did it matter what she did?

"Lani, he wants to make sure you understand what's going on with him. He doesn't exactly have a choice about leaving."

"I understand," Leilani said, wishing Betty would just drop the subject.

Betty eyed her suspiciously. "I'm not so sure."

"Hey," Leilani said as she backed away. "Don't worry. I'll be fine."

"Okay, if you say so. Jeff really does care for you. He doesn't want to make you unhappy."

I'm sure, Leilani thought. *And that's why he's letting his sister break it to me gently.* She'd found another flaw—he couldn't do his own dirty work.

Everyone was ready for the party. Now all they needed to do was get in the car and go.

The group headed out for the beach, bringing big boxes of food they'd cooked for the party.

Jeff was already waiting at the beach. When Leilani pulled into the parking lot, he was leaning against his rental car, watching the road. The instant he saw them, he pulled away and started walking toward the entrance to the beach. Leilani felt as though her heart would fall out of her chest.

"We'll get the food, Lani," Betty said. "Go talk to Jeff."

"Are you sure?" she asked.

"Of course. Now go on."

Jeff watched her walk toward him, a smile slowly creeping across his lips. No matter how upset Leilani was, she couldn't hold back her happiness at seeing him again, even though it could be for the last time.

Chapter Eight

"Y̶ou look beautiful as usual," Jeff said as she drew closer.

"Thanks, Jeff," she replied. It was all she could say. Nothing else came to mind; she was rendered speechless. The only thing Leilani could do was stand there and look at the most unique man she'd ever met, the man who was able to liven up any group of people with his warm smile. He was the man who'd captured her heart and was now about to break it by leaving Hawaii.

He tilted his head and studied her carefully, making her squirm. When his gaze met hers, she tried to blink, but her eyes felt frozen open.

"Lani, please come closer," he whispered, reaching out to her. He was leaning against a bench, and it looked like it might support her if she needed something to hold onto, so she took another step toward him.

"Jeff, I—" she began before he touched her lips with two fingers, hushing her.

"Please don't talk, Lani. I need to explain what's going on." His expression grew serious. "There's nothing I want more than to stay here for the next week. But I can't. Business—"

Now, it was Leilani's turn to interrupt. "No Jeff, don't," she said with more strength than she felt. "Let's just have fun tonight, then when you leave we'll have wonderful memories."

"I—" he began again.

"Please Jeff, no." Leilani knew that if he succeeded in explaining, she might break down in front of him. Reaching her hand out for him to take, she squared her shoulders, cleared her throat, and said, "Come with me to the party. We'll eat, dance, and have fun. After tonight, well, who knows?"

He blinked a couple of times, then nodded. "Okay Lani, it's a deal."

Although she felt like her happiness was about to walk out the door each time she thought about Jeff leaving, Leilani managed to have fun by forcing herself to live for the moment. She joined several of the other local women and did an impromptu hula dance, then she coaxed Jeff into the center of the group, showing him how to move his hips in time to the music.

They laughed like a couple of school children for hours. Jeff surprised her when he picked up a uku-lele and began to play a couple of classic Hawaiian tunes he'd learned from his old college buddies. It was a night to remember, one that Leilani was certain never to forget.

Then, Jeff did what she'd been dreading all evening. He turned her toward him, tilted her chin up, and said, "I have to go now, my sweet Leilani. My plane leaves in a couple hours, and I have to return the car."

Leilani gulped. It was that time. That time she thought she could will away. She wanted to start over and go back to the beginning, because she knew she'd lose her heart when Jeff boarded the plane back to the mainland.

"I'll be back," he said with certainty. "I promise."

She just nodded. Leilani closed her eyes as he dropped another sweet kiss on her lips. When she opened them again, he was gone and out of her life, just like that.

It seemed like no one noticed his absence at first. She stood alone and stared off into the distance while the aching sensation in her heart grew deeper. But when Leilani turned around she saw Betty watching her. Their eyes met, and Betty took that as her cue to come to her.

"You'll be okay, sweetie," Betty said tenderly, almost like a mother would. "Besides, he'll be back."

"Yeah, I know." Leilani knew her voice was monotone, but she couldn't muster any enthusiasm. In fact, she felt dead inside.

"I'll be surprised if he stays away for more than a couple weeks." Betty had her arm around Leilani, pulling her back toward the crowd. "Come on, Lani, we have guests. Let's try to forget about men who break our hearts, okay?"

Nodding, Leilani managed to fake a smile. Surely, Betty knew there was no way she'd be able to have fun now. But she could put on a show for everyone else. Betty was well-rehearsed at that. Late at night, during one of their many talks this visit, Leilani had learned that Betty's sacrifice of her relationship with Anthony still played over and over in her mind. When Leilani had asked her if she had any regrets, Betty hesitated then shook her head. "Things have a way of working out like they're supposed to." Leilani logically agreed, but her heart was breaking, and she had doubts.

After Jeff left, the night seemed to drag. Funny how those first hours together had gone by in a flash.

When it was time to go home, Betty asked Leilani to help her with the tables. "The man who rented them to me said to fold them and leave them leaned against the pole. He'll pick them up first thing in the morning."

Someone offered Jeff's friends a ride, so they said their good-byes and left. Betty looked at Leilani and smiled. She understood.

The two of them worked in silence, collapsing the legs of the tables, while the rest of the roommates packed up the food. A couple of the musicians stuck around to help. Once everything was where it was supposed to be, the roommates piled into Leilani's car and headed back to the castle.

"I'm exhausted," Betty said, yawning once they got home. "But I sure did have fun. There's truly no place like Hawaii."

"You got that right," Sally agreed. "In fact, I think I'll do what's in my heart and find a way to get back here. You only live once, and this is where I want to be."

"Seriously?" Betty asked enthusiastically. "Me too. Let's find a condo to rent, and we can be roommates again."

"Yeah!" Deanne exclaimed. "And we can hang out and have fun just like the good old days."

Betty laughed and Sally grumbled, "The good old days might not be so much fun in this good old body."

Everyone joined in the laughter. "Anyone want something to eat?" Sally asked as she shoved the last of the food into the refrigerator.

"You *are* kidding, right?" Deanne said.

"No." Sally pulled a banana off the counter, peeled it, and bit a huge chunk off the end. She was comical looking with her hamster cheeks puffed out, full of banana.

"You always were a bottomless pit," Betty lamented as she headed down the hall to the bedroom. "If I ate this late, I'd blow up like a balloon."

That night, Leilani managed to go to sleep faster than she thought she would, but when she awoke, she felt like a part of her had died the night before. She felt empty and alone, even with a house full of friends.

"I think I know how you feel, Lani," Betty said. "But you'll get over it."

"I'm not so sure about that." Leilani sat up and rubbed her eyes, hoping the stinging sensation wouldn't give way to tears.

"Sure you will. You just have to find something to keep you busy."

"Like what? We still have another week and a half before school starts again." Leilani let her long legs dangle from the edge of the bed. She didn't feel like doing anything today.

"Why don't we go for a drive to the Pali Lookout?" Betty suggested. "It's been ages since I've been up there."

"Okay," Leilani agreed. Betty was a guest, and she wanted her to have fun.

Sally wanted to walk along Kalakaua Avenue, the road that ran parallel to Waikiki Beach. Deanne had to work since she hadn't been to the surfboard stand in a couple days. And Terri and Marlene were sleeping in, something they hadn't done since Sally had arrived.

So it was just Betty and Leilani in the little car, driving up the highway to the Pali Lookout. "I've always loved this drive."

"Too many cars," Leilani commented. "It used to be much nicer, my mom said."

"I'm sure it did. But I still like it anyway. Look over there." Betty pointed to a waterfall in the side of a cliff that cascaded down to the foliage below.

Leilani had grown used to the tropical paradise, but she still saw the beauty that the tourists saw. That was why she could never imagine herself living anywhere else.

When they got to the parking lot of the Pali Lookout, Betty struggled to open her door against the strong wind that was always blowing there. "Do you think the legend of royalty is true?" she asked Leilani.

Leilani shrugged. "I have no idea, but it sure does make a nice story."

"Imagine if it was true, being able to jump off the cliff then being blown back up by the breeze, just because you're of royal descent." Betty's eyes were widened with a look of awe.

Leilani smiled, in spite of her aching heart. "I can only imagine. I haven't got an ounce of royal blood in me, I'm afraid."

"Tell that to my brother," Betty quipped. "As far as he's concerned, you're a princess."

Leilani didn't know what she expected, but she certainly didn't think Betty would bring up Jeff so easily. After all, wasn't she trying to help Leilani get her mind off him?

"I hardly think he sees me that way," Leilani said, shuddering from the cool, crisp breeze. She folded her arms and rubbed them.

"Oh, I think he does." Betty edged closer to Leilani and gently put her arm around her. "Jeff is in love with you, you know."

"Then why did he leave?" Leilani asked, turning to look at Betty. She wanted to know how someone could just ignore his feelings and rush back to his business as Jeff had.

"Business," Betty said.

"Couldn't it wait?"

"I'm not sure what the urgency was, but I do know one thing," Betty began.

"What's that?"

"If there's any way humanly possible, my brother will be back here before you know it, at least to see you. I know I still tease him about his womanizing ways of the past, but that's all behind him. Much to my surprise, he's turned into a very responsible man, and he won't neglect his responsibilities."

Leilani nodded. He might not neglect his business obligations, but he certainly didn't tend to the heart very well.

They stood there and stared down at the three cities spread out below them before getting back into the car to head back to town. "Man, I love this place," Betty said once again. "If I can't get a transfer back, I'll have to think about moving and looking for a job once I get here."

"You're really going through with that?" Leilani asked.

"Darn right, I am," Betty replied with a quick smile. "I've already made up my mind."

"But what about your family?"

"They'll get used to it. Besides, my parents love to vacation here. It'll give them a place to stay. Those hotels on Waikiki are so expensive, they can apply that to air fare and be able to come twice as often."

"Yes, this is true," Leilani stated. "But what about Jeff? Don't you two live close to each other?"

Betty turned and smiled at Leilani. "Maybe that won't change."

Leilani was confused. When she came to a light, she turned and gave Betty a puzzled look, but Betty was deep in her own thoughts about something, probably the idea of moving back to Hawaii.

"Betty," Leilani started with a little hesitation.

"Yes?"

"I'm not sure if this is a good thing to bring up, but I've got a question."

"Sure Lani. What is it?"

"What really happened between you and Anthony?"

"I told you."

Leilani paused as she looked at her friend's sad eyes. "I have a feeling you're leaving something out."

Betty looked stricken. She sucked in a breath and closed her eyes, making Leilani wish she hadn't asked.

"You don't have to tell me if it's too painful."

"No Lani, that's okay. I want to tell you." Betty licked her lips, turned to Leilani, and began talking. "Anthony and I were very much in love. He even started talking about marriage. It scared me, even though it shouldn't have."

"But why?" Leilani asked. "If the two of you loved each other, then marriage would have been logical."

"You'd think so," Betty said with a sarcastic grin. "But I wasn't that smart at the time. I had big dreams of having a career where I could really make something of myself."

"Well, isn't that what you did?" Leilani asked.

"Yeah, and look at me now. Anthony pined for me for about a year, but I wasn't even off the island yet when he decided to go back to his old high school sweetheart. I s'pose it worked out fine for him. Jeff says his wife is a really sweet woman who loves Anthony enough to make him happy. But here I am, working at a job I enjoy but stuck on the mainland." She sucked in a breath and slowly let it out. "I have family in Arizona, but I don't really feel like it's home anymore—not after living in Hawaii."

"I'm sure you'll find something here," Leilani said as comfortingly as she could. "There are lots of banks in Honolulu."

"Let's hope my company allows me to transfer. That would be so much easier."

They remained silent until they got back to the house. It was afternoon already, and no one was home. Terri had left a note on the counter saying that Jeff had called, but she didn't say whether it was for Betty or Leilani. And all it said was that he'd arrived safely.

At least he's safe, Leilani thought. Now she could stop worrying about him, something she hadn't realized she was doing until now. She let out a sigh of relief.

"I'm sure you'll see him again soon," Betty repeated.

"That's okay," Leilani said. "I'm an adult. I can handle this."

Betty snorted. "I don't care how grown up some-one is, a broken heart is awful. No one handles that kind of pain well."

"I never said I'd handle it well," Leilani pointed out. "I just said I'd handle it. And there is a differ-ence, you know."

"Boy, do I," Betty blurted out.

The next week went by so fast it surprised Lei-lani. She'd expected time to drag now that Jeff had left the island. But she suspected Betty made it her mission to keep her busy so she wouldn't have the time to pine for him.

Deanne had to work, so Marlene and Terri went with Leilani to see Betty and Sally off at the airport. "It's *aloha* good-bye for now, but we'll be saying the hello kind of *aloha* soon."

"I sure hope so," Marlene said. "I want both of you back as soon as you can get your transfers."

"Don't you worry," Betty said. "I'm coming the minute I have the chance."

"Me too," Sally added.

Marlene, Terri, and Leilani dropped *leis* over their friends' heads. Then, they stood back and watched as the women went through the gates and boarded the airplane.

Turning to Leilani, Terri asked, "Do you really think Betty will be back?"

Leilani shrugged. "I'm not sure, but I do know she's serious about wanting to come back."

"I hope she's able to do it," Marlene said. "We'll all be together again."

"That would be nice," Leilani agreed as they walked out to her car to head for home. One thing Leilani knew for sure was that things would never be the same, even if they did have all their friends on the island.

School started the very next week. It would be nice to get back into a routine, mainly so she could forget about Jeff. He'd been in every thought of hers since he'd stepped off the plane two weeks ago. Maybe she'd get so wrapped up in her studies, she wouldn't have time to think of him.

No such luck. Jeff was still in her mind, popping up at the most unexpected of times. In fact, once she even thought she saw him at the snack bar in the student union. But when the guy turned around, she saw that it wasn't Jeff. Her heart sank to her toes.

Each day went by, and she began to give up hope of ever seeing him again. He hadn't called or e-mailed, and he didn't even bother to write her a letter or post card. It was almost as if they'd never spent all that time together. Leilani felt an empty spot in her heart that she wondered if she'd ever be able to fill again. She seriously doubted it.

But she would go on and try to make the most of things. Betty had done it after Anthony. She could do it after Jeff. Maybe, if she lowered her expectations in men, she'd be able to find someone once she graduated and began living on her own.

Leilani used to wonder what the man she'd fall in love with would be like. Naturally, she assumed that she'd meet Mr. Right, they'd both fall equally in love, he'd propose, they'd marry, and she'd live the fairy tale existence she imagined for herself. Now she knew that wasn't the way it happened. Her bubble had been burst. If she wanted to have a husband and family, she'd have to settle for less than what she really wanted.

Betty called three weeks later. She sounded excited. "I talked to my boss, and he told me to speak to someone in corporate personnel. They think they might have something in Honolulu for me by the end of the year!"

"That's great, Betty!" Leilani squealed. She really was happy for her friend. Maybe they'd be able to do a lot of fun things together.

"And Sally said she's working on her company too. Our dreams might come true sooner than we thought."

"Oh that would be so wonderful, Betty. Keep me posted."

"Uh, Lani," Betty said, her voice coming down in tone, "have you heard from my brother?"

Leilani felt a familiar thudding sensation in her chest. "No, why?"

"I was just wondering." Betty's voice sounded awfully suspicious. She knew something.

"What?" Leilani had to know what was going on, even if it was bad. "What about Jeff?"

"He hasn't called you?"

"No."

"That knucklehead. He's gonna be in Honolulu in a couple of weeks. I think he's supposed to call you."

"Really?" Leilani couldn't keep the excitement from her voice, in spite of the fact that she'd told herself he was out of the picture for her. She now knew that wasn't true. He would be in the picture as long as he wanted to be.

"Yes. He's going to give you a call to ask if the two of you can see each other. But he won't be there long," Betty warned.

Right now, that didn't matter. Jeff was going to call, and he was coming! That was all Leilani cared about. Even if he'd only be here a few hours, she knew she could settle for that.

Sure enough, Jeff called the very next night. She picked the phone up on the second ring. "Leilani, have you talked to Betty?" he began.

"Yes," she replied, doing everything in her power to keep her voice from sounding shrill with excitement. "She told me you're coming to Hawaii."

They talked for several minutes. Jeff gave her his flight arrival time and said he could rent a car and drive to her house.

"Are you sure you don't want me to pick you up?" she asked anxiously. She wanted to see him the minute he stepped off the plane.

He laughed with delight. "I'm positive. I'll need a car, anyway, so let me come to you this time."

Leilani had to take deep breaths and let them out slowly so she wouldn't hyperventilate after she got off the phone. Deanne walked into the kitchen and stared at her until she calmed down.

"I take it you heard from Jeff," Deanne said as she got a glass from the cabinet and poured herself some water.

"Yes," Leilani said with a smile that wouldn't leave her face. "How did you know?"

Deanne snickered. "Lucky guess. When's the big day?"

Leilani told her when he was supposed to arrive. Her voice went up and down, just like her heart. She couldn't remember ever feeling so happy.

"Just remember," Deanne warned. "He's going back, and you'll be left feeling like mud, just like last time."

"Yeah," Leilani said, backing off her high. "That's true. But I want to enjoy him while he's here."

"Also, I don't want you to forget your mind. You

still have some classes to finish before you go traipsing around with some guy."

"Jeff's not just some guy," Leilani argued.

"No," she agreed. "He's not. But you still need to finish what you started."

"Of course, I will," Leilani said with a frown. "But if Jeff asks me to run off into the sunset with him, I won't turn him down."

Deanne's chin dropped, and she stared at Leilani. It was an awkward moment before she recovered.

"Just remember that your goal is to be the first person in your family to finish college," Deanne said as she backed toward the door.

After Deanne left the kitchen, Leilani thought about their conversation for a few minutes. Deanne seldom tried to rain on her parade, so she must have been acting like a fool over Jeff.

Leilani decided then and there that she'd cool off before Jeff arrived. She didn't want to make him think she was a total idiot over him.

Chapter Nine

On the date of Jeff's arrival, classes seemed to drag. She felt like a small child on the first day of summer vacation when her last class ended.

Since the house was so close to campus, Leilani seldom drove to the building where some of her classes were, but today was different. She had to run a few errands before going home, so she took the car.

The sky had been slightly overcast when she'd started out this morning, but now the sun was shining. The ocean breeze had been blowing all day, so she knew it would clear up.

Leilani had a hard time keeping her mind on her errands. She was eager to get home and shower before Jeff arrived. Glancing at her watch she saw that she still had several hours before she should expect him.

Finally, she managed to get everything taken care of, including splurging on a manicure. Today was different. It was special. She wanted to look her best for Jeff.

By the time she got home, no one was in the house, which pleased her just fine. It was much easier to shower and pick up the clutter when she was alone.

The phone rang just as she was stepping out of the shower. She quickly wrapped her robe around her and tried to catch it before the caller hung up. After all, what if it was Jeff?

It was Anthony. He wanted to know when Jeff was due to arrive.

"Tell him to call me as soon as he gets there," Anthony told Leilani. "He was supposed to stay here with us, but we have an unexpected visitor, and I'm afraid he'll have to make other arrangements."

"Oh, okay," Leilani said, frowning. This would be really inconvenient for Jeff, but she was sure there was somewhere else he could stay.

She went back to her bedroom, and the phone rang again. This time, it was Betty. "Jeff there yet?" she asked.

"No, where are you?" Leilani asked, feeling her excitement grow.

"Arizona," Betty replied. "Have him call me as soon as possible. I need to talk to him."

"Okay," Leilani replied.

After she got off the phone this time, she thought about how real it now seemed that Jeff was coming.

It took her about ten minutes to put on a dress and sandals. She had washed her hair, but she just let it air dry while she picked up all the books and magazines that were scattered throughout the house. Then, she washed the few dishes in the kitchen sink and put them away.

An hour later, Leilani heard the sound of a car pulling into the driveway. She tried to hold herself back, but she couldn't. She was too excited.

Just as he was getting out of the car he'd rented, she flung the door open. He stopped in his tracks and stared at her.

Leilani felt a warmth spread through her insides. Seeing Jeff was an incredible experience. She'd been able to fool herself for the past few weeks, telling herself that she really didn't care for him all that deeply. She'd told herself that she didn't know him well enough and that it was just infatuation. She wanted something she couldn't have.

But now that he was standing in her driveway, she knew that what she felt was real. It was the incredible surge of emotion she felt that let her know she cared for him deeply and that she wanted to run right into his arms and give him a big kiss.

She didn't, though. She just stood there and stared right back at him.

"Lani?" he said tentatively as he took a step forward. It looked like slow motion to her. Nothing seemed real at the moment.

"Jeff." She said his name, the sound of it like music to her ears.

They each rushed forward, and before she knew it, they were holding onto each other as if for dear life. Jeff rubbed her back softly and moaned. "I missed you so much, Lani."

"I missed you too, Jeff," she said as he lightly pushed her back to look at her. She knew he liked what he saw by the look of admiration in his eyes. "Oh, I almost forgot. You have to call Anthony and Betty."

"Betty's at Anthony's house?" he asked, looking very confused.

Leilani laughed. "No, but they both called." When he looked like it still hadn't registered, she added, "At different times."

"Oh," he said. "You had me worried. But then, Lani, when I'm with you I can't seem to think straight."

She laughed out loud with more happiness than she'd ever felt before. "I know exactly how you feel." Even though he was only visiting for a short while, Leilani was going to savor every moment with him.

"Mind if I use your phone to call Anthony?" he asked. "I can call Betty from his house."

"Yeah, call Anthony first, and if you need to call Betty, go ahead and do that too."

He went inside where she handed him the kitchen phone. "I'll be in the living room when you're finished with the call," she said.

She knew it was best to give him privacy while he talked with his friend and then his sister. Although she'd straightened the living room already, she moved a few things around and then turned on the TV. There was nothing else left to do.

When Jeff joined her in the living room, his eyes were glazed over. "What's wrong, Jeff?" she asked.

He was obviously bothered by something. Only a few minutes ago, he couldn't seem to take his eyes off her. But now he wouldn't look her in the eye.

"Nothing," he said in a clipped tone.

So that's the way it was, she thought. *He's suddenly clamming up.*

"Is there a problem you need to tell me about?" She wanted to give him one more chance to tell her, but she suspected he wouldn't.

"No, but my plans have changed. I won't be staying with Anthony."

"You do have another place to go, don't you?" Leilani was concerned. She knew the hotels were always booked months in advance, especially during this busy season.

"Kimo said I could stay at his place."

"At least you have someone else you can stay with," she said, a sense of relief flooding her. "Did you call Betty?"

"Yeah, I called her," he shrugged. "Wanna go somewhere and get something to eat?"

"Sure," she replied. "Let me get a sweater."

Although it was generally warm during the day, many restaurants had their air conditioners turned to cold. As Leilani went to her room to get her sweater, she thought about how quickly Jeff had changed. He seemed downright moody. Okay, so there was another flaw.

"Ready?" she said as cheerfully as she could when she came out and joined him.

He nodded, but he didn't say a word.

As she quietly studied Jeff, she saw a brief flicker of joy, but it faded quickly. He looked away shortly after she entered the room. Why was he acting like this when only minutes ago he'd acted like he wanted nothing more than to be with her? It had happened after the phone calls. What had Anthony and Betty said?

Each time their conversation became personal, Leilani noticed how Jeff would tighten up. He'd square his shoulders, tense his jaw, and look away, almost as if he wanted to shut her out. That hurt her more than anything he could have said. Obviously something was wrong. Why wouldn't he tell her?

Did he not trust her enough to let her know what was bothering him? Or worse, was there something about her that upset him?

Finally, after making herself crazy with wonder, Leilani decided to take the plunge and ask. "Jeff, did I say or do something to upset you?"

He looked directly at her, at first with a softness that warmed her heart. Then a veil lowered over his face, and he shook his head. "No Lani, I just have a lot on my mind."

"Business?" she asked, her head tilted forward, her eyes having to peak from beneath her eyebrows.

"I suppose you can call it that," Jeff nodded. Then he looked away.

This wasn't just moodiness she saw. Something had come up that he didn't want to discuss.

Jeff swallowed hard. Leilani looked so beautiful and vulnerable, sitting across the table, obviously worried about the way he was acting. Why couldn't he at least act like nothing was wrong? Just because Betty had told him to keep his distance after talking with Deanne was no reason for him to act like a jerk.

After spending time with Leilani when he was in Hawaii, he knew that he was in love with her. In fact, he suspected he'd been in love with her for a long time because he'd had a hard time keeping up that big brother act with her when Betty still lived at the castle. Even back then he'd wanted to kiss those naturally rosy lips and touch her hair that hung in silky strands down her back and shoulders.

Back then, though, his life was up in the air. He had just received a degree in computer programming and several offers from large corporations. However, he had no idea where he'd wind up. Now that he was in business for himself, he still didn't know for sure, but he'd tested his corporate skills and knew he had what it took to be successful.

Ever since his last visit, he'd decided he was going to move back to Hawaii. He was determined to do it soon, in fact. But it hadn't been nearly as easy as he'd thought it would be. His largest client wasn't willing to work with him from that distance, so he needed to find some Hawaiian clients, or at least clients who could work with him from across the ocean.

He had one client who was based in Hawaii, and that was one of the reasons he was able to justify this trip. And tomorrow, he had an appointment with another prospect. If they decided to do business with him he would be able to move back to Hawaii very soon.

The thought of being close enough to Lani so he could see her every day delighted him. That is, until he talked to Betty. Apparently, his sister had gotten a phone call from Deanne about Leilani. Betty warned him to keep his distance, at least until she graduated. She'd said, "Deanne seems to think you'll be putting Leilani's graduation at risk if you don't keep your distance." She wouldn't let him hang up until he promised not to allow his relationship with Lani to get too serious until she was done with college.

"Okay, I'll wait a few months," he'd promised her. And Jeff Sorenson never broke his promises, no matter how hard they were to keep.

Had he been wrong to start the ball rolling this soon to get back to Hawaii? Should he have waited a few months, at least until Leilani was closer to her graduation date? Jeff had wanted to be back in Hawaii since the day after he left, but now he wanted it to happen fast so he could be with Lani. However, he didn't want to be responsible for her not finishing her coursework. It meant too much to her.

When he first met her, his sister had warned him. "She's off limits to you now, Jeff. Leilani's one of those conscientious people who won't get into a serious relationship until she graduates. She's afraid she'll lose her focus and not finish school." He should have remembered that the last time he was here.

But he'd let his own emotions and desires get in the way of common sense. Now he needed to take a few steps back so they could get their lives in order before pursuing a romantic relationship with each other. His only fear was that she might lose interest if he backed off too far. *How far was too far?* he wondered.

Lani looked hurt when he didn't say much. He knew he was acting different, and it was hurting him to do it. He still needed to see her, to be with her. If he could return the friendship to the way it was before his last visit, perhaps their romantic relationship could be postponed until she was finished with school.

They ordered steaks with a salmon-tomato appetizer. This was Jeff's favorite kind of food, but he wasn't hungry. Nothing seemed right when he couldn't reach out and touch the woman he wanted more than anything in this world. His needs and desires had to be put on the back burner, but once that situation changed, he'd make sure he had Lani, and then he would never let her go.

Leilani tried hard not to stare at Jeff while they ate, but she couldn't help it. She'd noticed how his face changed expression, almost by the second. He went from looking thrilled to see her to unhappy to be with her. What was going on with him? Had he lost interest? If so, why had he even bothered to come to her house and ask her to dinner?

"How's school this semester?" Jeff asked politely. He was pushing the steak around on his plate and acting like he really didn't want to be there.

Leilani shrugged. "It's fine. I took most of my difficult classes already, so I'm able to coast a little bit this term."

"I always liked semesters like that," he said, nodding. "But with the computer programming major, I had to take a bunch of things that seemed totally pointless." Their conversation felt stiff and formal.

She forced herself to smile and wondered if he could see how miserable she was inside. "Everyone has to do that."

They made several more futile attempts at conversation, but it became apparent that it was pointless. Finally, Jeff stood up and said, "Time to take you home. Since I'm staying with Kimo, I need to get a move on. He's expecting me soon."

"Okay," she replied.

They walked to his rental car together, not saying a word to each other. Leilani felt as though she had a ton of bricks in her chest. Was there any way to bring back the magic between them? She still felt the same attraction, even more than before. But there was something holding him back. There was a wedge between them.

He drove slowly to her house, stopping in the driveway. Leilani decided to just come right out and ask him again what was going on.

"Please tell me, did I say something to upset you, Jeff?" she asked.

"No," he replied. He pounded his open palm on

the steering wheel, then turned and looked at her. "You've never said anything wrong, Lani."

"Then what's bothering you?" Her chest felt as if it would explode from fear of what he might say.

"The timing is all wrong for us," he replied with pain etched in his voice. She could tell it was an agonizing thing for him to say.

Reaching out and touching his arm as gently as she could, Leilani spoke. "I don't know what happened to you, Jeff, but I don't agree. Timing doesn't just happen for people. We have to decide what's right at any given time. Does this have anything to do with your business?"

He hesitated for a few seconds before he nodded. "I have a few loose ends to wrap up before I can see you again, Lani."

"I understand," she said softly. Now her head was beginning to feel light as her heart grew heavy. She needed to get inside. "Call me when you're ready, Jeff."

Leilani knew he was watching her as she went inside. He waited for almost a minute before he put the car in reverse and backed out.

As she stood in front of the window and watched him leave, she knew that part of her soul was going with him. Leilani loved Jeff Sorenson, and there was nothing she could do to stop her feelings for him. Everything seemed right when she was in his arms, and nothing could make her happy when she wasn't. She wanted this man to love her as much as she loved him. What could she do to make it happen?

The first thought that occurred to her was to leave Hawaii and follow him back to the mainland. Maybe if he saw her in his own world back home, he'd know he couldn't live without her.

But no, she couldn't do that. She'd come too far to quit school now. Her parents were counting on her, and they'd poured too much of their energy and money into college for her to let them down. She'd have to wait. Then, once she graduated, she'd find a job in Arizona and show him how much he needed her. His business was obviously important to him, so she'd find a way to fit into his life.

So what if he'd broken a few hearts in the past? If that ever happened to her, she could deal with it. But she wanted a chance to see how good they were together first.

So what if all attention was on him? That was just fine with Leilani. In fact, she'd much rather it be that way than have people staring at her.

And so what if he liked to be in control? He'd already shown he could hold back and behave without having to prove his point when Sally showed up.

Leilani wanted to follow Jeff wherever he went, all the way to the ends of the earth if necessary. Betty might not like it, but that was just too bad.

Chapter Ten

Leilani loved Hawaii, and she had no desire to move away. But if she had to make a choice between living in her favorite place in the entire world and being without the man she loved, or living anywhere with Jeff, there was no contest, she'd move.

In spite of the way he'd acted, Jeff came by two more times before he went back to the mainland. He always watched her closely, almost as if to memorize her features. Then, he slowly turned away, like something about her bothered him. She wondered what it was, but when she tried to ask, he just shook his head and said he had other things on his mind.

When he left a week later, Leilani found herself moping around the house. Deanne came into the living room where Leilani had been reading a magazine.

"Are you okay, Leilani?" Deanne asked as she leaned against the door frame.

"I'm fine," Leilani answered, not looking up from the magazine. Her eyes were still swollen from the cry she'd had the night before.

"You look pretty sad." Deanne continued to stand there, staring.

Leilani shrugged. "It won't be long before I'm finished with school. I've been thinking about moving to Arizona when I graduate."

"What?" Deanne shrieked. "I thought you had no desire to ever leave Hawaii. In fact, you once said you felt an obligation to stay close to your parents since you were all they had to take care of them in their old age."

"They're still young, in their forties. There is plenty of time before I have to worry about them getting old." She scrunched her nose as she mentally did some math. "Let's see, I'm twenty-two. I can get a job and retire in twenty or twenty-five years. Then I can come back and help my parents once I get it through my thick head that Jeff and I aren't meant to be. My parents will get the best part of me. Only problem is, knowing them they'll be running all over the world, having the time of their lives in their sixties. But I'll be here for them," she sniffled. "Probably single and miserable."

"B-but . . ." Deanne stuttered, but she didn't say anything. Leilani glance up and saw a look of anguish on her face.

"Hey, don't worry. I'll finish school and find someone to take my place here."

"That's not the problem. What about looking for a job in Hawaii? You said there were several possibilities for things in this area." Deanne actually looked desperate as she talked.

"I'm sure there'll be something in Arizona," Leilani said with a shrug.

Deanne held her hands up and took a few steps closer. "But what about Jeff?"

"What about Jeff?" Leilani asked, her eyebrows raised as she looked at Deanne. Any time Jeff's name was mentioned, her nerves tingled.

"What if he moves back here?"

"Ha!" Leilani wanted to say something pretty harsh, but she didn't want to upset Deanne any more than she already was. "That's not likely. I've heard his big account on the mainland refuses to work with him if he comes here. His business is too important to him."

"But what if he finds a way to work here and moves anyway?" Deanne pressed.

"I'll deal with that if and when it happens. In case you haven't figured it out, the only reason I'm thinking about going to Arizona is because Jeff is there. I thought he really cared for me, but he's acting so strange." She'd already revealed how she was feeling, so she figured she might as well bare all. "I fell in love with Jeff, probably a long time ago. But it only just came to light when he and Betty were here. I think he felt something, too, but now he's acting really weird around me. I figure that if I move to Arizona to be close to him, perhaps I can become friends with him, and we could get back to where we were before he started acting weird. Then maybe we can start over in our relationship and let things grow again. I know it's a long shot, but I'm willing to take the risk."

Deanne flopped back onto a chair. "You really do love him, don't you?"

Leilani looked her squarely in the eye. "Yes, Deanne, I love Jeff with all my heart."

"Oh, man!" Deanne exclaimed as she slapped her forehead with her palm.

"What?" Leilani asked, now really curious about her housemate's very odd behavior.

Deanne looked at her like a mongoose who'd been caught in the garbage. "N-nothing."

"Tell me, Deanne." For some odd reason, Leilani knew this had something to do with her and Jeff.

"You'll hate me for what I did."

"No I won't," Leilani said through clenched teeth. "Tell me."

Deanne inhaled deeply, then let her breath out in

a long sigh. "Oh, all right. I called Betty and told her what you said."

"What I said?" Leilani crinkled her forehead as she tried to remember what she'd told Deanne that would bear repeating to Betty. She had no idea.

"Yeah, you said you'd run off into the sunset with him if he asked you, and that worried me." Deanne looked terrified.

"I don't see why that would upset Jeff enough to act the way he acted while he was here."

"He doesn't want you to quit school."

"He thinks I'm gonna quit school?" Leilani asked in disbelief. "Did he say that?"

"Well no," Deanne admitted. "But the way you said it had me worried, so I called Betty."

"And she told Jeff I was gonna quit school?" Leilani was still puzzled how all this fit together.

"I don't think she said that in so many words, but—"

Leilani shook her head. "Deanne, I think it's sweet that you cared enough to call Betty, but I hate to be the one to tell you that what happened between Jeff and me—whatever it was—has nothing to do with anything you might have said. He's not the type to let hearsay cause him to react."

Deanne shook her head. "I just hope I didn't mess anything up for you. I really care about you, Leilani, and I know how important it is for you to finish college."

"Yes," Leilani agreed. "It is very important. And I fully intend to leave here with a college degree in my hand."

"But you're sure you want to leave?"

"Not really," Leilani admitted. "But I'll do whatever it takes to see what there is between Jeff and me, even if it means moving away from the place I love."

"I understand," Deanne said softly.

"Just promise me one thing," Leilani said as she stared directly into Deanne's eyes.

"Sure, anything." It was obvious that she felt bad, so now was the time to get a promise from her.

"Don't breathe a word of this to anyone. I don't want to risk having anyone try to talk me out of moving to Arizona. Since Jeff hasn't found a way to move here, I'm going there, and I don't want anyone to stop me."

"But—"

"Promise me," Leilani interrupted.

Deanne glanced down at the floor, then looked Leilani in the eye. "Okay, I promise."

"Good," Leilani said as she hopped up off the sofa. "Let's get something to eat. I'm starving."

Now that she'd had a chance to get that burden off her chest, Leilani felt much better. And she was glad to see that her appetite had returned.

They snacked on some leftover sushi and some

crackers from the seed store. "You know, they don't have food like this in Arizona," Deanne said.

"I think you can find sushi in Arizona," Leilani said as she took a swig of ginger ale.

"But these oriental crackers won't be available in every grocery store. You'll probably have to find a specialty shop to get them."

Leilani shrugged as a strange feeling tugged at her heart. She loved the things she was used to, but she loved Jeff even more. If she had to do without something, she figured food would be something she could give up.

At least now Leilani had someone to share her thoughts with. Deanne knew what she was going to do. Although Leilani hadn't planned to tell anyone about her decision to move away from Hawaii, she figured this would be okay. It gave her someone to discuss things with, to get them off her chest.

When Marlene came in from class, she quickly changed into her swimsuit and shorts, on her way to meeting some friends at the beach. She didn't have much time to chat, so she just exchanged greetings with them and left.

"Please remember your promise," Leilani said to Deanne after Marlene was gone.

"Trust me, Leilani," Deanne whispered. "Wild horses couldn't drag your secret from my lips. I've already learned my lesson about keeping my mouth shut. I'm really very sorry."

Leilani leaned over and gave Deanne a hug. "Hey, don't worry about it. No big harm done. In fact, you might have done me a favor. It made me think through things, like about what I want to do with the rest of my life."

Deanne snickered. "I don't like to think that far ahead. Gives me a headache."

"Yeah," Leilani agreed. "Me too."

Spending days in class and evenings thinking about what she'd do once she graduated didn't sound like much, but it took up most of Leilani's time. She wished she had someone to help her with her plans, but she knew that if she opened up to people, someone would try to talk her out of leaving Hawaii. In fact, after Deanne had a chance to think about their discussion, she'd told Leilani that she wasn't so sure it was a good idea.

But as time went on, Leilani became even more determined. She had one more break before her last few weeks of classes. She decided to take that time to start working on resumes. However, a phone call from the mainland halted that plan.

It was Betty. Terri answered the phone and talked for a couple of minutes before she held the phone out to Leilani.

"Betty wants to talk to you, Leilani."

"Hi Lani," Betty said as soon as she got on. "I'm coming to visit again, this time to look for a place to live."

"You got the transfer?" Leilani shrieked. "That's wonderful!"

"Well, it's not a done deal yet, but I want to start looking for a place to live."

Leilani was so happy for her friend, she thought she'd burst. "You know, you're welcome to stay here as long as you need to."

Betty belted out a hearty laugh. "Thanks for the offer, Lani, but I'm not sure how long I can handle sleeping on a futon."

It was tempting to tell Betty that she could have her place in the house once Leilani graduated, but she didn't. Betty didn't need to know yet about her plans.

"Oh, and Lani," Betty said, sounding like she had an afterthought.

"Yes?" Leilani asked.

"Jeff will be with me. He didn't want me to tell you. He wanted it to be a surprise. But I thought it would be best to warn you, just in case . . ." Leilani held her breath and waited. Betty didn't finish her sentence.

"Just in case?" Leilani prompted.

Betty let out a breath. "Just in case you needed to brace yourself."

Leilani giggled nervously. "Brace myself?" *Why would I need to brace myself?* she wondered. Was something going on with Jeff that she needed to know about? "Why?"

"Oh, I don't know," Betty replied calmly, almost as if she hadn't said anything that would set off alarms. "He really wants to see you, but I told him it might be best if he waited."

Now that Leilani knew what Deanne had told Betty, she was able to speak with some confidence. "I'd really like to see him too. Jeff is very special to me, even if things don't work out between us." Those were hard words to say, considering what she planned to do.

"Yes, Lani," Betty said with a softness that Leilani had come to appreciate. "I know."

When she hung up, all eyes were trained on her. "Well?" Terri asked.

"They'll be here on the first day of break. I'll pick them up from the airport," Leilani said, holding back some of her excitement.

"Sure you don't want me to see if I can find another way to get them here?" Marlene teased. "After all, I'd hate for you to go to this much trouble after you did all the driving last time they were here."

"That's okay," Leilani said with a lighthearted chuckle. "Picking them up from the airport will be my pleasure."

Once again the days went by slowly. Leilani found herself looking at the calendar, then the clock, counting days and hours.

Finally, she was finished with her last class at noon, right before break began. She had to study some this time, since the vacation was right in the middle of the semester, but she didn't mind. In fact, she figured it would give her something to help ground her, to keep her from floating too high above the clouds while Jeff was here.

The four roommates did a little extra grocery shopping. After the shopping trip, they brought the food home, then left to get some fast food like they always did. Deanne had started the tradition when she made the comment that after spending an hour in the grocery store, she didn't feel like cooking. So they left and went to their favorite fast-food joint with the largest variety of dishes.

"I can't believe you only have a few weeks before graduation, Leilani," Deanne said. "You're the youngest one of the group, so I feel very protective toward you."

"You can still watch over her," Terri said. "She's not going anywhere. In fact, I've been thinking that there's no need for her to move out of the house, since she's probably gonna have a job here on Oahu."

Leilani and Deanne glanced at each other, but quickly looked away. This was proof that Deanne had kept her promise so far and hadn't mentioned Leilani's plans to anyone. If she had, surely Terri would have been the first to know.

While they were out, the roommates went to Leilani's parents' house and picked some plumerias from the yard that was filled with all sorts of lush tropical plants.

"Thanks, Mrs. Kahala," Terri said as she sat down on the grass and began to string the flowers on the thread Leilani's mother had provided. It took them only a few minutes to make the *leis* for Betty and Jeff.

"You'll have to bring Betty and her brother by to see us this time," Leilani's mom told them. "We missed them last time."

"Okay Mom," Leilani said, bending over to give her mother a hug and a kiss.

They returned to the castle and went to work cleaning the place. It was spic and span within a half-hour, so they were able to go for a walk, then settle down for a game and conversation, something they did often. It was comforting to Leilani to have these people in her life. She'd lived with them for almost two years, and she imagined this was what it was like to have sisters. Only better, maybe, because they'd chosen each other.

That night, they went bed early. Betty and Jeff were due to arrive shortly before noon, so Leilani had plenty of time to shower and get ready.

Marlene and Terri were still asleep when she left the house. Deanne was awake in her nightshirt, but she said she had to go to work and wouldn't be home before dark. It was a busy season for tourists, and the owner of the stand preferred having Deanne working there because she had a good way with mainlanders, and they always came back a second time after dealing with her. Her boss said she was good for business.

Leilani felt her nerves twitch underneath her skin. She stood at the terminal and held the flower leis on her wrists, wishing Jeff and Betty were there already. The anticipation was about to drive her over the edge.

Finally, the plane landed, and the passengers started to walk through the gate. Leilani thought she'd never see Jeff and Betty, until she spotted his blond hair as he rounded the corner.

Her heart skipped a beat. When he looked directly at her, his face lit up, his eyes crinkled and his beautiful white teeth shone against his tanned skin. This was the man Leilani loved with all her heart. She could never give up on the possibility of a future with him.

Chapter Eleven

"**L**ani!" Betty exclaimed when she saw her old friend.

Next thing she knew, Leilani was being hugged by both Jeff and Betty, who backed off after a few seconds. "Here," Leilani said as she lifted the *leis*, first over Betty's head and then Jeff's. *"Aloha,"* she said, and kissed each of them on the cheek.

Jeff didn't let go of her after the kiss with the *lei*. He held on tight. Leilani couldn't help but notice the warning glance Betty shot his way. He just smiled back at her.

"Lighten up, sis," he said with a crooked grin, his arm now draped around Leilani's neck.

She couldn't remember ever feeling so attached to someone. But of course she'd never been in love before, either. Whatever had been bugging Jeff the last time he was here seemed to have disappeared. He was back to his old self again.

"We have a few more weeks for clearance," Betty said with another glance at her brother, which Leilani now understood. Then, Betty relaxed a little and added, "Lani, have you decided what you're going to do after graduation?"

Leilani didn't want to let the cat out of the bag, so she nodded. "I've got some ideas, but nothing definite yet." What she didn't say was that two companies in Arizona had expressed quite a bit of interest in her coming to work for them. She wanted to surprise him. She'd already met with the department heads after the campus recruiters had discovered her interest in moving to the mainland.

"Good," Betty said, looking down at her. Then she glared at her brother. "Isn't it good, Jeff?"

Leilani decided to take the bull by the horns, change the subject, and ask them about their trip. "How was the plane ride?"

One side of Jeff's mouth tilted upward, and his eyes fell droopy. "I tried to sleep a couple times, but motor-mouth here didn't want me to."

This definitely was the old Jeff she'd fallen in love with. He had a way of teasing Betty in a good-natured way. And Betty could toss back a comment without it sounding like a mean-spirited fight.

"I had things to say," Betty said in a playful huff. "Let's get our bags."

Leilani noticed the sign language between Betty and Jeff, but she decided it was just something brothers and sisters did. So she tried her best to overlook it as they made their way to her car.

"I'll come back and get a rental car in the morning," Jeff said. "Anthony's wife said she'd bring me over here."

Leilani noticed that Betty didn't get that wistful look on her face this time, when Anthony's name came up. In fact, she smiled. "Do you think they'd mind if I came over and saw the babies?"

"Are you sure you're ready for that?" Jeff asked tenderly. His voice had changed, and the love he had for his sister was evident. It warmed Leilani's heart.

Betty thought for a moment, then nodded. "There's something about babies coming into the picture that changes everything. I want Anthony to be happy, and he obviously is. It's time for me to get on with my own life."

"Yeah," Jeff agreed. "Time for you to pursue another love interest."

"What's wrong with that?" Betty asked as she playfully shoved her brother into the front seat of Leilani's car.

"Absolutely nothing, baby sis." The look he gave Betty held a gentle warning.

"I'll drop off Jeff at Anthony's place first," Leilani said. "We can stop at the beach and see Deanne on the way home too. She wants to see you."

"Good," Betty said. "She sent me an e-mail saying she wanted me to meet the hunk who just started working with her a few weeks ago."

Leilani laughed, and Jeff snorted. "Oh no," he said, "not again."

"What's wrong with Deanne enjoying herself at this time of her life?" Betty asked from the backseat as Leilani wound her way out of the airport parking lot.

"Nothing Betty, absolutely nothing." Jeff turned and looked out the window as they drove past rows and rows of cars. "Just remember that later on in the week."

"Don't do anything stupid, Jeff," Betty said softly, barely loud enough for Leilani to hear.

"You worry too much," he replied. "My promise only holds until June."

"Yes, I know. Just don't forget your promise."

"Have I ever?" he asked. He shifted in his seat uncomfortably and fidgeted with the collar of his polo shirt.

"No, I guess not," she replied.

Leilani listened and wondered what kind of promise would only be good until June. She hoped it had to do with her, but maybe not. It could be related to business, knowing Jeff.

Anthony was standing outside when Leilani pulled up in front of his house. She resisted the urge to turn around and give Betty a look of consolation.

She was shocked when Betty hopped out of the car, took a couple of strides toward Anthony, and reached out to shake his hand. He took her hand, pulled her to him, and gave her a brotherly hug. Leilani noticed his slight hesitation, but when Betty started talking, he visibly relaxed. They stood on the front lawn, smiling and chatting.

Leilani got out of the car, since it appeared that Betty might be there for a while. "How are the babies?" she asked.

"You should see them," Anthony said with pride. "The girl looks just like her mother. And the boy is the spittin' image of my dad, bald head and all."

Betty stepped toward the house. "I'm dying to get a look at them. Do you think your wife would mind?"

"Of course not," he said as he ushered them all inside. "She'll be glad you wanted to see them."

Leilani met Anthony's wife, Pua, and instantly liked her. She had long dark hair with streaks of red where the sun had bleached it. Her eyes were large and almond-shaped, and her skin was a little darker than Anthony's. She looked like someone who'd be pictured on a Hawaiian tourist brochure.

The baby girl was named Malia, and Anthony

was absolutely right. She looked so much like Pua it was amazing.

Kale, the boy, was bald and had an animated expression on his face. He was a living doll.

"She's beautiful," Betty said with a sigh as she stared down at Malia. Then, she looked at Kale and cooed. "He's sweet too."

"Thank you, Betty," Pua said with warmth. "Come back and see us any time you want to. I have a feeling I'll be here a lot, now that we have Malia and Kale. They have a way of keeping me from going out too much."

"Yeah, they have a schedule for everything," Anthony said in awe, like Malia and Kale were the first babies in the world. "A feeding schedule, a sleeping schedule, and the diaper changes." He pinched his nose and fanned his face with the other hand. Everyone laughed.

"I'm sure you don't mind," Jeff spoke up. "Malia and Kale are beautiful babies."

"Don't get too attached while you're here," Anthony warned good-naturedly. "They may call you uncle, but that's as close as I'll let them get."

"That's fine," Jeff said. "I've always wanted to be an uncle."

Leilani saw the grimace on Betty's face, but she didn't say anything. She just touched Betty's arm and said, "We need to go now. Deanne's waiting for us."

"You okay?" Leilani asked Betty as they pulled away from Anthony's house.

Betty nodded. "It went a lot better than I expected. That first time seeing him after splitting with him was hard, but the ice has been broken." She grew quiet for a few seconds before adding, "I like Pua. She and Anthony make a great couple."

Leilani cast a glance at her friend and nodded. "I agree. They seem perfectly suited for each other."

They stopped off at the surfboard stand to meet Deanne's latest flame in her long list of guys. Leilani had to admit Lui certainly was nice looking. During the brief conversation they had, it became apparent that his only purpose in life was to catch the next wave. But Deanne grinned from ear to ear when he looked at her. At least he was a nice diversion for her at the moment, Leilani thought. Deanne didn't like being without a guy for very long.

"She knows how to pick 'em," Betty said as they drove away.

"He is cute, but kind of without direction," Leilani added.

"That's an understatement." Betty glanced out her window for a moment, then turned back to Leilani. "Speaking of direction, have you narrowed down any plans at all for after graduation?"

Leilani shrugged. "I figure I have plenty of time to decide, but yes, I have options."

"Wanna tell me about them?" Betty asked, her expression filled with hope.

With a swallow, Leilani replied, "Not really. I need to work through a few things in my own mind first."

From the corner of her eye, Leilani saw Betty chew on her bottom lip, as if something was bothering her. "Just make sure you go through with graduation."

Of course she'd go through with graduation. She hadn't come this far to quit. Surely, Betty knew Leilani was smart enough to follow through with graduation, which was only weeks away. Something else must have been bothering Betty. She decided to go easy on her friend.

"Don't worry about me, Betty. I'll be in that graduation cap and gown, and I'll be the happiest one at the ceremony."

"Good," Betty said with relief. "I don't want you to do anything foolish." She was beginning to sound like a broken record.

They got Betty settled in Marlene and Terri's room. Last time, Betty wound up staying in Leilani and Deanne's room the whole time rather than switch like she'd planned, since Sally was also staying at the house. Betty said she didn't want to wear out her welcome, so she even offered to sleep in the living room.

"No way," Terri told her. "It's our turn to have you for a week."

Since they had a lot to do, and Jeff was supposed to meet with businessmen in Honolulu for dinner, the women decided to eat snack foods instead of cooking. The refrigerator was loaded with groceries they'd bought the day before.

"Wow!" Betty said as she opened the refrigerator door. "I've never seen this thing so packed."

"We wanted to make sure you had plenty to eat," Marlene said.

"You must think I'm a pig." Betty pulled out some cold cuts and started stacking them on a platter she'd gotten from the cupboard. It wasn't long before the table was piled with all kinds of food, from bread to sushi to *lomi* salmon to pineapple slices. It was a fabulous Hawaiian feast—eclectic and delicious.

Conversation flowed without a hitch. The women were comfortable around each other, and they never lacked for something to say. It saddened Leilani that this was coming to an end in several weeks, but it was inevitable. They couldn't go on being roommates for the rest of their lives. Still, she knew she'd remember times like this with fondness and nostalgia.

The next morning, Leilani was in the kitchen eating a muffin when the phone rang. She grabbed it before it rang a second time to keep from waking anyone. They'd stayed up late the night before, so this morning they were sleeping in. Betty had an appointment with her bank in Honolulu to interview with the local board members, but it wasn't until mid-afternoon.

"Lani?" Jeff's voice came through the line clearly.

"Hi, Jeff." Her heart did that familiar flip-flop. It happened so often, she was getting used to it by now.

"Wanna go to the beach this morning? I have to meet with someone late this afternoon, but I have a few free hours and I'd like to spend them with you."

Of course she wanted to go to the beach with him. She'd go anywhere he wanted her to go, right now. "Okay, Jeff," she said as lightly as she could. "Want me to pick you up?"

"No, Pua drove me to a rental car place, so I can drive."

They made plans before Leilani hung up. She really didn't mind taking her car, but Jeff had told her before that he didn't want to take advantage of her generosity. Besides, she suspected he was nervous about riding in her rattle-trap. She knew she'd have to sell it before she moved to Arizona, and she really didn't mind. Once she had a job and a place to stay, she'd get a newer, nicer car.

Leilani couldn't remember ever having a better time in her life. All they did was swim; the waves weren't big enough to bodysurf. But Jeff gave her his undivided attention, and he took advantage of every opportunity he had to kiss her. They must have kissed at least a hundred times.

Still, she felt he was holding back. His kisses were sweet, but he kept pulling away and mumbling to himself. She figured he must be stressed out over a business deal, but she didn't want to ask. If she pushed too hard, he might clam up and start acting like he had last time she'd seen him.

He brought her home early enough so he could get ready for his appointment. Leilani kept hoping he'd ask her out for dinner, but he didn't. Instead, he suggested going out the next night. She jumped and said, "Yes!"

Jeff's warm smile at her reply made her tingle inside. Whenever he looked at her, she melted and wanted to pull him to her. But she refrained from doing so because she still wasn't totally sure about his feelings for her. She knew she'd be taking a huge chance when she moved to Arizona. It was a chance she felt like she had to take, if she was to know what could be between the two of them.

Jeff was about to go insane with wanting to talk to Leilani about his plans. But he'd promised Betty he'd wait until the woman he loved graduated, and not a second sooner.

Jeff and Betty had grown up knowing that their

mother had regrets in her life, one of them being that she'd dropped out of college during her last year to marry their dad. Sure, they had a wonderful marriage, but once Jeff and Betty left the nest, their mom was restless.

Betty often encouraged her to go back and finish her degree, but she just shook her head. "No, I'm fine. It would be a waste to spend all that time and money on myself when I'm happy with things the way they are," their mother would say.

Jeff knew that she wasn't totally happy and that most of what their mother felt was fear. But he didn't say a word. He just hugged his mom and told her she was the best.

After Betty's discussion with Deanne about Leilani, Jeff knew what was going on in his sister's mind. She didn't want Leilani to act on emotion right now, at a time when she was most vulnerable. Jeff suspected Leilani wouldn't do what his mom did. Besides, she was only weeks away. Still, he'd promised to keep quiet about his plans, and he wasn't one to go back on his word. What were a few weeks, anyway? He'd be living here soon, and he'd be free to take this relationship with Leilani as far as she was willing to go.

He closed his eyes and saw the blissful scene he kept playing over and over in his mind. It was filled with Leilani and him, together, looking forward to the rest of their lives.

In less than six months he'd be living here again, and hoped to be making plans for their wedding. Of course, he'd propose to her the minute he stepped off the plane, before he moved into the condo for which he'd signed a lease.

Back when he still lived in Hawaii, and he'd first met Leilani, Betty told him to back off. During the few dates he'd had with Lani, she had done things to him no other woman had managed to do. She'd found a place in his heart and etched her image into his mind. He sometimes felt driven to the point of insanity with wanting her.

"I love you, Jeff," Betty had said, "but I also know your history."

"I really care about her," he'd argued.

"Good," she said quickly. "Since you care about her, you'll wait until she finishes school to date her."

He couldn't argue with his sister, who seemed so wise. Betty had never acted as impulsively as he had, and now she acted like she didn't trust him. Jeff had to admit, her worries were justifiable. He had quickly lost interest in every woman he'd dated before. But they were nothing like Leilani.

This visit of Jeff's was even better than his first one, which gave Leilani hope, and made her believe that her plan would work to her advantage. Leilani lived for the hours she'd spend with him in between his numerous business meetings. He must have quite a company back in Arizona to have so many contacts here, she thought. She figured that this would give her an opportunity to visit her parents once she left Hawaii. That is, if she and Jeff stayed together after she moved to Arizona.

Although she knew Jeff's time in Hawaii was limited, she also knew she had something really big to look forward to. Moving to Arizona would require a lot of work on her part. She hoped Jeff would be happy about it. But she didn't want to say a word to him until her plans were finalized.

Leilani gave Jeff a kiss right before he boarded the plane. Betty still had a few more days of meetings at the Honolulu branch of her bank, so she would fly back later in the week.

Since Leilani hadn't told anyone besides Deanne of her plans to move, she decided to do a little investigative work to see what Betty thought of the idea without giving her the specifics about what she was going to do. She wanted some feedback.

"How do you think I'd like Arizona?" Leilani asked Betty one afternoon when the two of them were sitting around, having lemonade.

"You'd love it," Betty replied with no hesitation.

"Is housing expensive?"

"It's a heck of a lot cheaper than here," Betty

said. "But it's all relative. People there complain just like they do here."

"How about the people?" Leilani glanced down at her hands that had begun to shake. She wanted so badly to tell Betty, but she didn't want to come right out and say anything just yet. "Are they nice?"

"Very nice. In fact, I'm sure you'd love the people there." Betty was smiling back at her with a questioning look. "Why are you asking? Thinking about moving to Arizona?"

Leilani shrugged and glanced away. "Never know what I might do."

"Wouldn't that be funny?" Betty asked. "You move to Arizona and I move here. There's irony in there somewhere." She was quiet for a moment, like she was sorting through something in her mind, before she added, "But I'm sure you wouldn't move to Arizona. Your place is here."

"Yeah," Leilani said. She needed to change the subject before she spilled the beans and told Betty what she was going to do. "What time is your meeting today?"

Betty glanced at her watch and replied, "In a couple of hours. I sure do hope we're able to work this out. Moving back here is all I can think about."

"I know what you mean," Leilani said.

Leilani had to force herself to be patient and let things happen at the right time. She'd graduate, book her flight, and contact a place in Arizona that specialized in short-term rentals. Then she'd go on the interviews with the companies who'd expressed an interest in her during campus recruiting, which had gone very well for her.

One of the personnel recruiters had told her that her degree in general business was perfect because they preferred their new hires to be open to their training. Another corporate executive said that general business majors were usually more diverse in their knowledge, so they could be placed wherever they were needed. Leilani was glad she'd picked such a broad degree. Her options were wide open.

Betty didn't have much time left on the island, so Leilani and the other housemates took every opportunity to be with her. She promised that she'd be back for good, if possible, within the next six months.

"I certainly hope you're able to pull this off," Terri said, hugging her good-bye.

Marlene nodded in agreement. "We'll all be glad for that."

Leilani drove Betty to the airport. Right before Betty moved toward the final gate, she turned to Leilani, hugged her, and said, "Somehow, you and Jeff will get together one of these days. Trust me on this."

Leilani smiled, wanting more than anything to tell Betty what she was about to do. But she didn't. She needed to keep it to herself, just in case it didn't work out.

Jeff was ready to close on his latest deal. He'd managed to acquire the account of the largest pine-apple canning plant in Hawaii, and he'd been re-ferred to a couple of small computer firms that needed a consultant. He'd found another program-mer to take over his Arizona account, so he was finally free to move back.

Now, all he had to wait for was Leilani's grad-uation. The fact that she only had weeks to go brought a smile to his face. Man, she'd be surprised to find out he was moving back for good.

Jeff's initial plan was to rent a condo until he and Leilani made their relationship permanent. Once they came back from their honeymoon, they'd start looking for a house to buy—one that would be big enough for a family.

Leilani graduated at the end of May, and he was moving to Hawaii in August. He'd wait until right after her ceremony to tell her his good news. He would have already let her know if he hadn't made that ridiculous promise to Betty. But he was always true to his word, it was something he prided himself on.

*   *   *

It was graduation day, and Leilani couldn't have been happier. Every surface in her room supported a bouquet of flowers, from her parents, her grandparents, her cousins, and everyone else who knew how much this meant to her. She'd put the arrangement from Jeff on the kitchen table so everyone could enjoy the three dozen red and white roses he'd sent. She'd never seen a more beautiful bouquet.

"That cap and gown actually look good on you," Terri said as she stepped back to admire Leilani. "It made the rest of us look like penguins."

"Yeah, too bad Jeff couldn't make it to the ceremony," Marlene added. "But those flowers are to die for."

Everyone gave Leilani a hug before she took off for the auditorium where the ceremony was to take place. They were all going to attend, but they didn't need to leave for a couple of hours.

Leilani was happy about graduation, but that didn't even come close to how she felt about seeing Jeff in two weeks. She'd already booked her flight to Arizona, and the rental agent had called and told her she was holding an efficiency apartment in a very nice section of town. Leilani was especially thrilled that it had a nice little patio garden right outside a sliding glass door.

She still hadn't mentioned a word of her plans to anyone besides Deanne, and she was bursting to share them. Tonight, during the celebratory dinner, she'd tell her parents, whom she hoped would give their blessing. Then, she'd tell her housemates in the morning.

The two companies she was scheduled to visit on a final round of interviews had all but told her she had the jobs if she wanted them. Now, all she'd have to do was pick which one was more suited to fulfill her career goals. And of course, she'd discuss it with Jeff.

Chapter Twelve

"**S**he what?" Jeff yelled into the telephone after reaching Deanne in Hawaii.

"You heard me. She left three days ago for Arizona. She moved there."

"She can't do that."

"Oh, but she can and she did. We tried to stop her, but she was determined to be near you." Deanne paused for a second before she went on. "Please don't hurt her, Jeff. She's a precious person, and if you break her heart, so help me, I'll—"

"Don't worry about me breaking her heart, Deanne," Jeff barked. "I've got to talk to her and make sure she doesn't take one of those jobs."

"I take it you don't want her there?"

"No, I don't. She has to go back." Jeff felt like

177

his chest had opened up and his heart had fallen out.

Deanne sighed. "That's what I was afraid of. She moved there to be close to you, but you don't want her like that."

"That's not it, Deanne," he said. "I do want her with me."

"Then what's your problem, Jeff?" He heard the impatience in her voice. "You're not making a bit of sense."

"I won't be here much longer. I just signed a lease for a condo in Honolulu. I'm moving back in August."

"Oh," she said, dragging out the single syllable. "Now I get the picture. You'll be two ships passing in the night."

"Not if I can help it," he said bluntly. "Now tell me how to get in touch with her."

"I-I'm not supposed to even tell you this much, Jeff. Leilani will be furious and she might fuss at me."

"That's nothing compared to what I'll do to you if you don't tell me." Jeff knew he sounded much worse than he could ever be, but he was a desperate man. He had to get hold of Leilani before she signed a contract for a job. Leilani was an honorable woman. She was the type to follow through on any commitment she made, even if it meant giving up a piece of her own heart. If she took one of those jobs, they might never get together, because she'd feel compelled to give them their money's worth. He loved Leilani's integrity, but he hoped it wouldn't work against her to keep them apart.

Deanne reluctantly gave him Leilani's number and address in Arizona. Jeff told her thanks, and then actually hung up on her.

He immediately dialed Leilani's phone number but got an answering machine. Glancing at his watch, he saw that it was two o'clock in the afternoon. He'd just have to go to the address Deanne had given him and camp out on Leilani's doorstep.

Jeff had to wait for a solid three hours before Leilani pulled up in front of the apartment. Since she'd moved, he knew she would have a different car, so he had no idea what to watch for. But that striking face with long dark hair got his attention right away as she pulled into her parking space.

She blinked a few times before she slowly opened her car door and got out. "Jeff?"

How did he know where to find me? Leilani wondered. She'd given explicit instructions to everyone who knew her whereabouts to keep it a secret until she was ready to tell him. She had no idea what she was going to say, so she just stood there and stared at him.

He slowly walked toward her, never once taking his eyes off her face. Was he angry? No, that didn't look like anger she saw in his eyes. Was he confused? As he drew closer, she saw that he looked very much in control and totally grounded. What was going on?

"Leilani," he whispered as soon as she was within reach. He pulled her into his arms and just held her, whispering her name over and over into her hair. It felt good to be in his arms, but she wanted to know how he found out where she was.

"Who told you?" she asked, pulling back.

"It doesn't matter," he replied. "But what in the world do you think you're doing?"

"I-I wanted to be closer to you, Jeff," she answered. "But if you don't want me here—"

"Darn right I don't want you here," he said, his voice hoarse and husky.

Leilani's heart felt as though it had broken in two. She looked down and nodded. "I think I understand, Jeff. I'll leave you alone if that's what you want."

"That's not what I said," he whispered in a gravelly voice. "I said I don't want you here."

"B-but—"

"I want you in Hawaii, with me."

Leilani quickly glanced up and looked into his eyes. She was confused. Did he know what that sounded like?

He let go of her for a moment and held his hands up like he was exasperated. "I do everything, including move heaven and earth, to find a way to get

back to Hawaii so I can be with you, and you go
and do something like this?"

"You're still trying to move back to Hawaii?" she
asked, her voice raising to a squeak.

"Yes!" he shouted. "And I have it all worked out.
I'm moving back in August."

"But what about your mainland accounts?" Leilani cleared her throat. "Will they let you work from
there? I thought—"

"I'm dropping my big account and picking up a
couple in Hawaii. What do you think I've been
working on during my visits?"

Leilani took a step back and blinked. She
couldn't believe her ears. Jeff was working toward
moving back, while she'd been trying to move to
Arizona? She felt a giggle rising in her throat, and
soon she was laughing uncontrollably.

"It's not funny," he hissed.

"No, it's not funny," she agreed. "It's hilarious."

"Did you take a job?" he asked.

Slowly, Leilani shook her head. "I've had a couple more interviews with two companies. They both
want me, but I've been having a hard time deciding
which one to choose. They both sound good. In fact,
I was going to call you next week to get some advice from you."

"I can give you some advice right now," he said
as he folded his arms across his chest and regarded
her with a wary eye.

"You can?" Did this mean he'd changed his mind and wanted her to stay here while he moved to Hawaii?

"Turn them both down," he stated flatly, leaving no room for doubt that he was serious.

"Are you sure?" she asked softly. "I'm in the final stages of interviews with both of them. If I turn both of them down now, I'll never get another chance like this."

Jeff tightened his jaw. Leilani watched as he sucked in a breath through clenched teeth, making a whistling sound. He looked highly perturbed.

Finally, he closed his eyes and opened them, leveling her with his gaze. "Okay, Leilani, you're forcing me to jump the gun. I didn't want to do this yet, since it's not the romantic setting I'd hoped for."

Now Leilani was completely confused. What was Jeff talking about?

He got down on one knee, right in the middle of the parking lot, and took her hand in his. "Leilani, I love you with all my heart." He paused for a moment and chuckled to himself, like it was a private joke. He looked down at the pavement. "I can't believe I'm doing this here," he mumbled. Then he gazed back into her eyes. "Leilani, I'll be moving to Hawaii in August, and it's not only because I want to live in Hawaii. I do love it there, don't get me wrong. But mainly, I'm coming back because I can't imagine spending the rest of my life without you."

Leilani felt her heart pounding a very irregular rhythm. "I feel the same way, Jeff, and that's why I'm here."

He kissed the back of her hand, turned it over, and kissed her palm. She managed to remain steady on her feet until he started kissing her fingertips, one by one, looking into her eyes as he did. She was afraid her knees would buckle, but he was right there. She had no doubt he'd catch her if she started to fall.

"Okay, Leilani, I'm going to ask you a very important question, and I want you to think about it until you're sure of your answer."

Her eyes widened as she looked down at him and nodded. She was still holding onto her purse and briefcase, and they were in the middle of the parking lot. She could only imagine how this looked. After a quick glance around, she realized they had a small audience, but she didn't care right now.

"Leilani," he said softly, taking her hand and resting it on his chest, right above his heart. "Will you make me the happiest man in the world and be my wife?"

If Jeff hadn't quickly stood up and put his arm around her waist, she would have crumbled right there at his feet. As he steadied her, she turned and whispered, "Yes, Jeff, I will." Then the tears began to fall. "But I still need some help with my decision."

He flinched. "Your decision to marry me?"

"No," she said, giggling deliriously. "My decision about how to tell the corporate people what my plans are." She crinkled her forehead. "What exactly are my plans. Jeff?" She wanted to make sure she had this straight before she made any mistakes.

Jeff turned her around to face him. He held onto her shoulders and looked directly at her, leaning down so his face was level with hers. "Okay, Leilani. I don't want to start our engagement by telling you what to do. But if you want my opinion, I think you should start over in this job hunting expedition. Turn them both down and interview with companies on Oahu. Honolulu has plenty of great businesses that would love to have someone as bright at you on their team."

Leilani felt a warm glow travel through her body. This was exactly what she'd hoped he'd say.

Betty stood in the dressing room of the small church with Leilani and her mother. "Just remember that Jeff can be stubborn at times," she warned. "If he insists on having his way, and it's not something you want, just put your foot down and tell him how it's gonna be."

Leilani and her mother exchanged an understanding glance. She turned back to Betty and nodded.

"I'll tell him you told me to insist on getting my way."

"And remember, you're about to become not only my brother's wife, but my sister as well. I'll always be here for you if you need me."

Leilani gasped. "Does this mean you got your transfer?"

Betty winked and nodded. "Looks that way."

The two women hugged, pulling apart when Leilani's mother nudged them toward the door. "Your father's waiting for you, Leilani. Betty, get into your maid of honor position."

Leilani was glad to have her mother and future sister-in-law there to guide her on the happiest day of her life. So much had happened over the past few months, her head was spinning.

Each of the housemates walked down the aisle, their bridesmaids dresses in different colors that flattered them. Betty marched down the aisle last, right ahead of Leilani and her father. Her pikake *lei* hung over her shoulders, framing her face, while she grasped her bouquet of white orchids tightly in her fist.

When she looked at the men lined up at the altar. Leilani's heart swelled with love. Her groom was wearing a leaf garland draped over his shoulders in the traditional Hawaiian royalty style. He looked wonderful as he gazed at her with love and tenderness in his eyes.

Leilani loved the blend of old Hawaii with the mainland traditions. It was symbolic of her wedding to the most wonderful man she'd ever known.

As they said their vows in front of family and friends, Leilani had no doubt she was doing the right thing. And she knew that the rest of her life would be filled with laughter, joy, and surprises because Jeff would make certain that she'd never be bored.